Chegwith Skillett Escapes

by the same author

ELLIS AND THE HUMMICK
THE ABRADIZIL
JEMIMA, GRANDMA AND THE GREAT LOST ZONE
THE AMAZING WITHERSPOON'S AMAZING
CIRCUS CREW
THE ROLLICKERS *and other stories*

Chegwith Skillett Escapes

ANDREW GIBSON

illustrated by Chris Riddell

faber and faber

LONDON · BOSTON

First published in Great Britain in 1995
by Faber and Faber Limited
3 Queen Square London wc1n 3au

Photoset in Palatino by Parker Typesetting Service, Leicester
Printed in England by Clays Ltd, St Ives plc

Andrew Gibson is hereby identified as author of
this work in accordance with Section 77 of the Copyright,
Designs and Patents Act 1988

A CIP record for this book is available from the British Library

ISBN 0–571–17114–1

2 4 6 8 10 9 7 5 3 1

*To Kirsty and Claire,
and to Barbara, hoping
she'll read one sometime*

Chapter One

Jeremy was playing with his catapult in the garden one morning when he saw a bottom. The bottom was sticking out of a window; a ground floor window in the house next door. The next door house belonged to the Bartholomews. But the bottom did not. It was not Mr Bartholomew's bottom. It was clad in loud check trousers. Mr Bartholomew never wore trousers like that. And it was not Mrs Bartholomew's bottom either. It was simply too small. Mrs Bartholomew's bottom was not small. It was not at *all* small. In fact, this was a stranger's bottom. And the stranger was probably up to no good.

Or rather: he *had been* up to no good. For now he was clearly stuck. The bottom was wedged there, held tightly in place by a window. And it wasn't going anywhere; the bottom, that is. Slowly, carefully, precisely, Jeremy took aim, and fired.

The bottom wriggled, feverishly. But it stayed stuck.

Jeremy climbed cautiously over the Bartholomews' fence. Obviously the Bartholomews

were not in. Otherwise they would surely have seen the bottom themselves. Cautiously, Jeremy approached the bottom. When he reached it, he inspected it at leisure. Then he inspected the legs. They were long, and rather spindly. Then he inspected the feet: they were cased in tattered, old black boots. Then he squeezed his head between the window and the sill and examined the chest and arms. They were wearing a dirty old patched black jacket that was much too short for them. Finally, Jeremy peered at the head.

It bristled with spiky, straw-coloured hair. The face was pallid. The nose was big. The eyes were wild, profound, funny and sad. The lips were moving. In speech.

'*Get me out of this*,' they said.

Jeremy thought for a while. Then, 'I don't think I'm going to,' he replied.

There was silence. Then 'Alas,' said the man, 'alas,' and he stared mournfully at the floor beneath.

'This isn't your house,' said Jeremy. He felt he had to apologize. 'It's the Bartholomews'. You're a stranger. What are you doing here?'

'I want two things,' said the man, squirming a little, 'and two things alone. I want to escape. Then I want to give up, and let that be that. But first I need my father's balloon. And my father's balloon is here somewhere.'

'A likely story,' said Jeremy, who was not a boy to trust a stranger right away.

'It isn't at all,' said the man. 'That is why it is sure to be true. In the eye of eternity, at any rate.'

'Eye of what?' said Jeremy. Matters – he thought to himself – were rapidly getting above his head.

'Eternity,' said the man. 'Do you know anything about eternity?'

'No,' said Jeremy.

'Me neither,' said the man. 'But what is unlikely today is likely to be likely tomorrow. Or if not tomorrow, the next day. That's what I believe, anyway. Now will you *please* let me up out of this?'

'No,' said Jeremy, still being firm.

They lay there for a few minutes, side by side. Then, 'Mr Bartholomew hasn't got any children,' said Jeremy, 'so there.'

'Of Mr Bartholomew,' said the man, 'I know nothing. Or rather, I know one thing: he is not my father.'

'Ahah,' said Jeremy.

'My father,' said the man, 'was named Skillett. Chegwith Skillett, like me. Unlike me, he is dead,' and a look of terrible grief crossed Chegwith Skillett's face, upside-down. 'I am sure of this, because Belvedere Jones braved my gaol and gaolers to inform me.'

'I knew it,' said Jeremy. 'You're a crook.' But the more he knew it, the less sure he was. And who

4

was Belvedere Jones? Maybe *he* was the crook.

'Criminals,' said Chegwith Skillett, 'are out for
their own ends, are they not?' Jeremy nodded.
'They go in search of rich pickings?'

'They do.'

'They seek out the cream on the milk?'

'That's right.'

'But I seek neither cream nor milk. I wish, not to
pick, but to drop. Simply: I intend to take my leave.
I have been here. I do not wish to stay. But *I have to
have my father's balloon.*'

Belvedere Jones, dead Mr Skillett, eyes of
eternity, gaolers, gaol . . . It was all a bit too much
for Jeremy. But since he was in fact not merely a
strong-minded but also a clever, imaginative,
unusual boy; and since he liked the unexpected
(and did not get nearly enough of it); and since
moreover he had decided that he rather liked
Chegwith Skillett, 'Can't you do something to
prove it?' he said. 'Prove that you're not a criminal,
I mean?'

'I can,' said Chegwith Skillett, 'but only if you set
me free. Then you can accompany me to the top of
the house, to the loft (which is where the balloon
will be); and you can watch me take the balloon
and *only* the balloon; and you can then watch me
leave the house forthwith; and you can, if you
please, accompany me again to the nearby park,
and stand witness as I assemble the basket, inflate

5

the balloon and then promptly ascend into the blue empyrean; never, never to be seen again.'

And he spoke with so much feeling and conviction; and seemed so desperate to be gone; that Jeremy really had no choice.

'But why do you think the balloon is here?' Jeremy asked, as they clambered rapidly up past Mrs Bartholomew's aspidistras, her flying ducks and her paintings of Torquay.

'I have not seen my father for very many years,' said Chegwith Skillett. 'But he left me a letter telling me where I could find his effects in case of his non-return. His effects – it seems – are mostly here, in the loft. He stayed here once for a few days (he was on the run, as I am now).'

'That must have been before the Bartholomews came,' said Jeremy. 'Before my parents moved here, too. But a balloon with a basket is a very big thing. How are you going to carry it yourself?'

'My father must have carried it *solus*,' said Chegwith Skillett.

'Unless he took a taxi,' said Jeremy.

'I don't believe he did,' said Chegwith Skillett. 'And what my father could carry *solus*, I shall be able to carry *solus* too. He was – you see – an extremely gifted inventor. He could for instance make things that looked small that turned out to be actually rather large. That, I suspect, will be the

6

case with this balloon. At all events – now we shall see,' and he pointed to a trapdoor above their heads.

'We can't get up there,' said Jeremy, at once.

'Why not?'

'We haven't got a stepladder.'

At which point Chegwith Skillett lay down rigid on the floor, his arms spread wide, and stared at the ceiling in frank disbelief.

'Woe,' he said, dully, after some time.

'I wouldn't stay there for very long,' said Jeremy, 'if I were you. The Bartholomews will be back in a moment. And in any case, I've thought of a solution.'

'What is it?' said Chegwith Skillett, still staring at the ceiling.

'I can get up on your shoulders. I'll go into the loft and get the balloon for you.'

Chegwith Skillett promptly scrambled up. 'You really will?' he said.

'What else would I want to do, in the Bartholomews' loft?'

'Lofts can be very interesting places. Especially for young boys.' Skillett eyed him, mistrustfully. 'But listen: the balloon will be in a large red bag. And there's a trunk, too. A small brown wooden trunk, with iron hasps. It contains the rest of what my dead Dad owned. As far as I know, at any rate.'

Skillett bent down. Jeremy sat on his neck. Skillett straightened up. Skillett tilted. Teetered. Swayed . . . then straightened again.

'Hold still!' Jeremy cried, fumbling with a bolt. He fumbled at a second; levered the trapdoor up; grabbed at the ledge, stood up, and hauled himself in.

'Have you found it?' said Skillett, after a while.

'Are you having trouble?' he asked, a little later.

'What of my balloon?' said Skillett, to the air.

'I swear,' said Skillett, 'that boys are not to be

trusted. Boys – to be plain – are brats. Boys are as undependable as the creation itself. If I had to name the meanest, most mischievous, most malevolent creatures on earth . . .' Jeremy appeared at the trapdoor. He was grinning.

'You're right,' he said. 'Lofts are really interesting. Do you know what I've found? There's a . . .'

'Where is the balloon?' Skillett roared.

Jeremy grinned again. Then he lowered a large red bag through the hole. Chegwith Skillett crowed ecstatically, and opened his arms. Jeremy let go.

Chegwith Skillett fell to the ground with an OOOF!, and lay supine in a cloud of dust.

'I wouldn't stay there for very long,' said Jeremy, 'if I were you. The Bartholomews . . .'

'Damn the Bartholomews!' cried Chegwith Skillett. 'Where's the trunk?'

Jeremy dragged a brown wooden box to the edge, and dropped that on Skillett, too. Then he swung himself down out of the trapdoor, picked Skillett up, helped him to put the bag on one shoulder, fixed one of his hands round a handle on the trunk . . . and then the two of them ran down the stairs, out of the front door, along the street, around a couple of corners, and into the local park.

They reached a tree and lay down at its base, giggling, out of breath. Then 'So,' said Skillett, 'my time is come. Goodbye to all. To the neat little houses and the leafy greenery. To the . . .'

'Mr Skillett,' said Jeremy.

'Chegwith,' said Skillett. '(*Not* Cheggie, or Cheg).'

'Why are you on the run?'

'I have fled my captors,' said Skillett, grandly. 'I have escaped their compound. Once and for all. But I fear that, even now, they are in hot pursuit.'

'So you *are* a criminal,' said Jeremy.

'Not in the slightest. I am a poor meek fellow, and much maligned.'

Jeremy thought for a moment. 'So you really need your balloon,' he said. 'To get right away, I mean.'

'That is correct.'

'Well,' said Jeremy, 'that bag is quite a big bag. But I don't think it's big enough to hold a balloon. Even a trick balloon made by a gifted inventor.'

'To be honest, I was thinking the same, myself. But I always had a very great faith in my father. I do not propose to relinquish it now. Whatever that bag may hold, it will be adequate to my purposes. As you are about to see,' and with those words, Chegwith Skillett got up, rushed to the bag, opened it, up-ended it, and dumped the contents on the ground. Then he fumbled in the heap for a while.

'This,' he announced, 'must be the balloon,' and he pointed to a mound of dusty cloth. 'And this must be the basket,' and he waved at a parcel of tightly-packed sticks.

'Hm,' said Jeremy. 'What about this?' and he picked up a small metal tube from the ground and pulled it out to its full length. It had a handle and a button and a trigger at one end. 'It looks like . . . a sort of collapsible gun.'

'It probably is,' said Skillett. 'I wouldn't fire it, if I were you.'

'Hm,' said Jeremy. 'But it looks like a walking-stick, too. That's what it is: a walking-stick. What do you think this is?' and he brandished a cube-shaped plunger in the air. 'And what's this for?' He pointed at a little flame-thrower. 'And look. A miniature barrel organ.' It was, too – a tiny, little barrel organ, with a handle that turned and played sweet, little, tinkly tunes. 'I wonder what *this* unlocked,' and he picked up a large, complicated, golden key. 'What was your father up to, with all these odd things?'

'I do not know,' said Skillett. 'I never knew what my father was up to. Sons seldom do, by and large. But that is of no concern to me now. What does concern me is' – and he rummaged in the mound of cloth – 'how am I to inflate this balloon?'

Jeremy came over. 'Very simple,' he said.

'I see,' said Skillett, 'very simple. You, a small boy, without any pump or similar gadget to hand, take one look at this obdurate, shapeless cloth, and you say, very simple. I, son of the gifted inventor himself . . .'

'You pull this,' said Jeremy, and he pointed to a cord, on which was a label that said: PULL TO INFLATE.

'Ahah,' said Skillett. 'Of course. Very well. I shall,' and he pulled, hard. And sure enough, there was a hissing sound, and a sucking sound, and a roaring sound, and a rumpety pumpety oomphy sort of sound, and there was a great big round balloon, standing there, just like that, and wobbling slightly. And had it not been for Jeremy's presence of mind – he snatched a line that was tied to the balloon and ran round the tree with it, several times – the balloon would have drifted clean away, and there would have been – perhaps – no story left to tell; or a different one, at the very least.

'Very good,' said Skillett, and he clapped his hands. 'And now for the basket . . . Um.' He contemplated the parcel. The parcel showed no signs of life. Skillett sighed. 'I am not a great one for baskets,' he said.

'Very simple,' said Jeremy.

Skillett frowned; opened his mouth; then shut it again, with a snap. 'I'm sure it is,' he said.

'You pull this,' said Jeremy, and he pointed to a very little lever, with a label on it that said: PULL FOR AUTOMATIC ASSEMBLY.

'Ahah,' said Skillett. 'But naturally,' and he pulled smartly on the lever. And there it was: a decent-sized basket. They fastened it to the balloon, put the various other objects in it, then stepped back and admired. The basket was neat and snug and had room for a small trunk and . . .

'Me,' said Skillett, hoisting the trunk into the basket. 'It is all the space I crave. To live in, that is. Otherwise, of course, I crave immense amounts. The more the better, my boy, the more the better. Pure space, infinite space, the great grand expanses that I hope . . .'

'You'd better head for them quick,' said Jeremy, and he pointed.

There, across the park, there were figures coming running. A man in a suit, a policeman with a dog, and several men in white coats. Skillett groaned, and covered his face in his hands.

'Alas,' he said. 'It is they, of course.'

'Who?'

'My captors. Plus a sundry other or two. But I shall defend you against them,' and suddenly – with a quite unexpected strength – he lifted Jeremy up from the ground and deposited him in the basket. Then he stood in front of the balloon, arms akimbo, one leg slightly bent, frowning, with lifted brow, and waited.

The men came running up. They looked red and out of breath.

'So,' said the man in the suit, panting fiercely, regaining his breath, 'Chegwith Skillett.'

'So,' said Chegwith Skillett, 'old Humpy.'

'Mister Humpidore to you,' said the man. 'We should never have let you out on those unwatched afternoon walks. But you promised not to climb the wall.'

'I didn't climb it.'

'Pardon me, but there is no other way out.'

'I *vaulted* it. With agility, gusto and magnificent aplomb.'

'Where did you get that balloon?'

'It's not mine,' lied Chegwith Skillett. 'It's the boy's. Boys do sometimes have balloons, you know.'

'Not that sort of balloon.'

'Actually,' said Chegwith Skillett, 'it's my father's.'

The man groaned. 'Not that again,' he said. 'Skillett – your father is dead.'

'I know,' said Chegwith Skillett.

'That's an improvement,' said the man. 'Yes, he is dead. He died very many years ago. But up until the present you have claimed he was alive. He was – you maintained – a traveller and inventor, but too busy travelling and inventing to come and see you. Now, however . . .'

'Oh, he's dead all right,' said Chegwith Skillett. 'But he didn't die very long ago. He died quite

14

recently.'

'How did he die?' said Jeremy, all at once.

'I don't know,' said Chegwith Skillett, mournfully. 'But I am sure that he is dead, because Belvedere Jones told me so.'

'Nonsense,' said Humpidore. 'Who?'

'Belvedere Jones. He's an inventor friend of my father's. My father had many inventor friends. He came to visit me in your abhorrent institution, and he told me.'

'*Stuff* and nonsense,' said Humpidore. 'You dreamt about him. Then you decided that your dream was true. You've always done that, you know. That's why you came to stay with us. Because you believe in your dreams. That's why you've got to come back with us now.'

The policeman edged forward with the dog; the men in the white coats, too. Casually, Chegwith Skillett took hold of the rope around the tree. Then he took a penknife from his pocket.

'If you come a step closer,' he said, 'I shall cut the rope, and this little boy will be gone.'

The men stood still. Then 'Jump for it, laddie!' roared Humpidore.

'I have had second thoughts,' said Chegwith Skillett. 'How could I have been so wantonly cruel. To think of leaving my poor small friend to such a solitary career.' He leapt briskly into the basket. 'I shall of course accompany him myself.'

The knife went slicing through the rope. The men dived . . .

And the balloon went floating, floating, slowly, peacefully, up above the telegraph wires, the trees, the chimneys and – in a very little while – the office blocks and pylons and radio masts; into the great, broad, spacious blue.

17

Chapter Two

For a long time, Jeremy gaped. He gaped at the shrinking criss-cross of roads. He gaped at the dwindling patchwork of fields. He gaped at a big, wide spread of sunlit sea. Then he turned round.

Chegwith Skillett was lying on the floor. His feet were on the trunk and his hands behind his head. He was staring at the sky. He had put – it seemed – the whole world from his mind. Including Jeremy.

'Is that all you're going to do?'

'It is. I intend to float interminably through the air,' said Chegwith Skillett, after a pause, 'doing nothing of anything but gaze.'

'But you can't just go on and on for ever in a balloon.'

'Correct. For mediocre, practical reasons, I shall have to touch ground from time to time. But I shall do so as seldom as possible, and only when there's no-one about.'

'There's *always* someone about,' said Jeremy. 'And what about me? You kidnapped me, you know.'

'Well,' said Chegwith Skillett, 'you'll have to get

used to staring at nothing, too.'

'But I don't want to,' said Jeremy. 'That means there's nothing to look at. And how about food? You'll have to eat and drink. Your eyes may be able to make do with nothing, but your stomach won't.'

'For drink there will be rain. And for food: among my father's effects (he said) there were always such things as *Rations* to be found,' and Chegwith Skillett took his feet off the trunk. Jeremy looked inside. He plunged his hands into piles of paper and assorted junk and there – sure enough – was a tin box which said – precisely – RATIONS (Containing ALL GOOD THINGS). Jeremy opened the box. It was packed with little, brown cubes. He put one in his mouth. It didn't taste like ALL GOOD THINGS at all. It was chewy and rubbery and tasted of nothing in particular. Nonetheless . . .

The rations were something to live on. So, every few hours, the two of them each chewed a small brown cube; as the sun went down, spreading red and gold across the sky; as the stars came twinkling to life; as Jeremy stretched himself out on the floor (which for some strange reason seemed always to stay warm); as the two of them blearily woke to a pale-green dawn; as a breeze snatched them and sent them racing into the clouds, along with the clouds, and away; as the rain soaked them and the sun dried them out; as hard, gaunt, snow-covered

mountains surrounded them, menaced them, let
them go. Quietly awestruck, they chewed.
Occasionally, Skillett talked, and Jeremy heard:

1 That he (Chegwith Skillett) remembered little of
   his life; but that he had been at Humpidore's
   Home for a *very* long time.
2 That in all those years – until the arrival of
   Belvedere Jones – he (Chegwith Skillett) had
   been visited only by his father (whom he
   adored).
3 That he (Chegwith Skillett senior), traveller,
   inventor and (presently) dead, had been a most
   mysterious figure, about whom little was
   known (by Chegwith Skillett junior, at least).
4 That he (Chegwith Skillett junior) was
   unanxious to learn about his father, because a)
   his father was just plain dead; b) he (Chegwith
   Skillett junior) wished (as Jeremy knew) to do
   nothing of anything but drift and gaze . . .

Which was what he did; and what he kept on
doing; and might have done for an appallingly long
and tedious time; in spite of all the questions which
Jeremy (who *did* want to know more about his
father) asked him; had it not been for the white
balloon.

It was on the second day that the white balloon
appeared.

It appeared as a dot on the horizon. But it grew,

and grew again. It was moving fast.

'Faster than we are,' said Chegwith Skillett.
'Down on the floor and hide. They'll think we're a
ghost balloon. Then they'll be scared and leave us
alone.'

'That's ridiculous,' said Jeremy. 'I bet they
spotted us ages ago.' But Chegwith Skillett was
already back on the floor – this time facing down,
not up. Reluctantly, Jeremy joined him.

They waited for a while. Then:

'Skillett!'

Chegwith Skillett trembled violently. 'It *can't*
be . . .'

21

'It is.'

'Humpy?'

'Who else could it be?'

'But Humpy does not possess a balloon (not to my knowledge, at least).'

'Skillett! Stand up! I can recognize your balloon! I know you're there, too!'

'It doesn't *sound* like Humpy,' said Chegwith Skillett.

'Skillett! Stand up! Or WE'LL BLOW YOU RIGHT OUT OF THE SKY!'

'However deeply loathsome Humpidore may be, he does not blow innocent, law-abiding do-nothings out of skies,' said Skillett.

'BLAAAAAAM!' Something whistled horribly over their heads.

'Last chance, Skillett! The next one's your balloon!'

'Well, I'm standing up,' said Jeremy, bravely, 'even if you aren't,' and he did.

It wasn't Humpy.

There was a white basket under the white balloon. It held three men. One was tall and thin. He wore a long, white coat. He had a thin face, with a pair of small spectacles on the end of his thin nose. He was carrying a loud hailer.

The others were smaller – burly and stout. They were standing to attention, like guards. They wore identical, little, black caps, and each of them carried an enormous blunderbuss.

They all three stared at Jeremy. They looked very surprised.

'*Who are you?*' roared the thin man, at last.

'Jeremy!' screeched Jeremy. 'Who are you?'

'*I am M'GRAW.*'

'*And I . . . am Chegwith Skillett!*' Suddenly, Chegwith Skillett's head poked up over the side of the basket. He had found a loud hailer for himself, in the trunk.

There was a pause. Then '*No,*' said M'Graw, '*you're not.*'

'*Unless,*' shouted M 'Graw, after another pause, '*Unless . . . you're the son.*'

'*The very same!*' roared Skillett.

M'Graw pondered Chegwith Skillett at length. Then, '*So what I have heard is true*?' he said. '*Your father is dead?*'

'DEAD,' sighed Skillett, roaringly, 'DEAD.'

'*How did he die?*'

'*I don't know.*'

'*Well . . . YOU'LL just have to tell us where it is!*'

'*Beg pardon? What?*'

'*Don't play the fool! Your father spent his life on it! He must have told you where it was!*'

'*I'm afraid I don't know what . . .*'

'*Out with it, now!* OR OTTO AND ERROL . . .' M'Graw waved right, then left. Otto and Errol lowered their weapons and aimed.

'*Where what is? I don't understand.*'

'*Skillett, don't lie. Your father was making a . . .*' but at that moment, there was a sudden gust of wind, and the white balloon went scooting off. Skillett and Jeremy ducked down again.

'*What* was your father making?' whispered Jeremy.

'I really don't know. And I really don't know how he died, either. All such matters are obscure to me.'

'Try to remember! Or we're going to be blasted to bits!'

'*Skillett!*' Jeremy stood up. The white balloon had drawn level again. '*I'll count to three. Tell us where it is, or die yourself. One . . .*'

Jeremy reached down quietly into RATIONS (Containing ALL GOOD THINGS). He picked out two of the cubes.

'*Two . . .*'

Jeremy took his catapult from his pocket, fitted a cube into the sling, and fired it. Then he fired the second, too. The first hit Errol on the nose. Errol dropped the blunderbuss and howled. The second cube missed. Otto glowered, and kept his aim.

'*Too bad, Skillett!*' bawled M'Graw. '*Thr . . .*' Then he stopped and stared. Otto stared. Errol stopped rubbing his nose, and stared. Jeremy stared, and Chegwith Skillett, too.

Four contraptions were wheezing and clanking and chugging towards them; the craziest contraptions you could hope to see. They had handles and wires and levers here, and pulleys and pistons and cog-wheels there; and they wobbled and wavered and swayed as they came; yet somehow they kept straight on course. And as they came, Jeremy heard shouts and gurgles of glee.

'WHOOPS! HIYAAAY! PEEP PEEP PEEP!'

Otto raised his blunderbuss; too late.

The contraptions were armed: with a popgun, a cannon, a slingshot and a bow. The pilot with the bow fitted in an arrow, and fired.

The arrow hit the white balloon. There was a flumping sound, then a hiss. The white balloon began to lose height.

'*Skillett!*' yelled M'Graw. '*Don't think I'm done! I'll be back on your trail! I must know where* . . .' His voice faded out. His balloon was lost from sight.

The flyer with the bow chased after him for a while. Then he came back. One of the other pilots threw a large iron hook into Chegwith Skillett's basket and started towing him away.

'Who do you suppose they are?' said Chegwith Skillett to Jeremy.

'How should I know? *You're* the one with the ex-flying father.'

'Speak respectfully of the dead,' said Chegwith Skillett, aggrieved. 'Particularly my dead,' he added, after a while.

They all journeyed on until they reached a sort of platform in the sky. It was quite as weird as the planes. It had a rusty, old garage at one end, and a rusty, old garage at another, and in between stood a clutch of battered huts. There were rusty, old cranes and a great, yellow windsock and poles and wires and metal masts. One by one, the planes went in, the last one gently, towing the balloon.

When they'd touched down, Jeremy and Chegwith Skillett got out, tied the balloon up, and waited. The flyers got out, too, took off their helmets, and approached.

At their head came a smart little woman, with bobbed blonde hair and bright red lips. 'Hello!' she said, at once. 'My name is Baby Doll Bette. I may not look like an air ace, but I am. So is he,' and she pointed to a great tall gangling man with a quiff and a guffaw. 'It was he who fired the arrow, just now. He is also our engineer.'

'Long Larry Lankin,' said the man, 'ahaw! Pleased to make your acquaintance, I'm sure.'

'So am I,' said a second little woman with a merry cackle and a wicked grin.

'This is Saint Theresa,' said Bette. She frowned a little. 'She is our daredevil-in-chief. Theresa will take on any challenge at all . . .'

'And rise to it admirably, too,' said Theresa. 'But I don't always agree with Bette,' she added. 'She thinks she's the boss . . .'

'I *am* the boss,' said Bette, stiffly.

'Whereas I think that we're all bosses. And above all me, when I feel like it.'

'And this,' said Bette, through gritted teeth, 'is The Chunterer,' and she pointed to a plumpish, hangdog figure with thick moustaches and a weary smile.

'Hn thn mnthn thn,' said The Chunterer.

'The Chunterer,' whispered Bette, 'is not at his best with words.' The Chunterer sighed, and gave Theresa a devoted, wistful glance. 'But he's just the man for a tight corner. When we're in trouble, it's

28

The Chunterer who turns up trumps. He always knows what to do.'

'Hm,' said Jeremy. 'How does he tell anyone else?'

'He has his ways,' said Bette. 'And he knows what to do and he has his ways because he's proud to be a member of . . . AERONAUTS ANONYMOUS!'

'Hn thn thn hrn,' said The Chunterer.

'As are we all,' said the other two.

'But who *are* Aeronauts Anonymous?' said Jeremy. 'I mean, what are you *doing* here?'

'I'll tell you,' said Bette, and she did. She took them into one of the huts, and, while Chegwith Skillett lay on the floor and stared at the ceiling, she told Jeremy how the four of them had once lived down below; and how they had tried to help people down below, too, because that was what they liked doing, and dreamt of doing well; but in the end they despaired.

'We did,'said Theresa.

'Wn thn,' said The Chunterer, eyeing her adoringly.

'We got tired of the low-down, crawling people.'

'Tired of the low-down, crawling earth.'

'So we decided to help the airborne, instead.'

'We made our planes.'

'We found our platform.'

'We came up here for good.'

'And we never went back.'

'*Found* your platform?' said Jeremy.

'That's right. Just found it, one day. You meet some strange inventors in the sky. One of them must have built the platform. Then he went, and left it. Which suited us fine.'

'Perhaps it was Chegwith Skillett's father who made it,' said Jeremy.

'Was he an inventor?' said Bette, to Chegwith Skillett. Chegwith Skillett said nothing. 'Your friend doesn't talk much,' said Bette.

'He doesn't talk *at all*,' said Theresa. She

prodded Chegwith Skillett with her toe. 'A *nutter*,' she announced. 'We've got a *nutter* on our hands, I'm afraid.'

'No you haven't,' said Chegwith Skillett, suddenly. 'My father was an inventor, yes. But I simply wish to have done.'

And then – since Chegwith Skillett said no more – Jeremy told Aeronauts Anonymous all he knew about the Skilletts, and about how he and one of the Skilletts came to be there, and about what M'Graw had said.

'Hm,' said Bette. 'So no one knows how old Skillett died.'

'Not so old,' said the son, from the floor.

'And he was making something special. Special enough for M'Graw . . .'

'To be very wicked indeed,' said Theresa, 'just to get his hands on it.'

'That means there's a mystery to solve.'

'A case,' said Theresa, 'for us.'

'This is not a case,' said Chegwith Skillett from the floor. 'Or if it is anyone's case, it is mine. And I wish only to neglect it.'

'But you,' said Theresa, 'are a *nutter*. You aren't responsible for your actions, or rather, lack of them. We must head out at once . . .'

'I'm the one who gives the orders,' said Bette.

'Ask for M'Graw's balloon . . .'

'All decisions are made by me.'

31

'Hunt him down, and get him to tell us the truth.'

'*Silence!*' yelled Bette. 'That is *not* what we're going to do.'

'It's what *I'm* going to do,' said Theresa, walking off, 'and I expect it's what The Chunterer's going to do, too. Chunterer!' The Chunterer looked after her, languishingly; turned back to Bette, who frowned, very fiercely; and scratched his head.

'*Chunterer!*' called Theresa, again.

The Chunterer ambled off. The others waited for a minute. Then they heard the sound of two contraptions taking off.

'She'll be back,' said Bette, briskly. 'She always comes back. With him right behind her, of course. Forget them for now. Let's get to work. Did Mr Skillett (the father, I mean) leave anything behind him which might help?'

Jeremy thought. Then he remembered. 'There are some papers,' he said, 'in a trunk.'

'I forbid you to look at them,' said Chegwith Skillett, not stirring. So Bette and Jeremy and Long Larry Lankin took the trunk from the basket and started looking at the papers.

The papers were covered in diagrams, figures and facts, and looked very clever and very weird. But they told you nothing of Chegwith Skillett's Dad. It was only when Jeremy and the others were almost done that Bette let out a cry. Jeremy peered over her shoulder. At the top of the paper she was holding, there was a note which read:

THE SURVEYOR: N !"£$%; E ˆ &*()

'Who's The Surveyor?' said Bette.

'No idea,' said Jeremy.

'He's someone, that's for sure. And someone important to old Skillett, too. Well – we know where he is on the map.'

'That's not a map reference,' said Jeremy. 'Map references have numbers.'

'To those who know a little about *my* sort of sky . . .'

'You what?'

'That passes for a map reference. And I can read it. Let's go.'

So they did. They lifted Chegwith Skillett back into his basket. Long Larry Lankin fixed the balloon up with a little engine, so it could keep pace with the two planes. He fixed it up with a little radio, too, so they could all talk to each other as they went. He showed Jeremy how to steer, and they all prepared to take off.

'Look!' said Jeremy. The horizon was brandishing great fists of dark cloud.

'I *defy* omens!' cried Bette. She marched over to her plane, and clambered into the cockpit. 'Ho, for The Surveyor!' she cried. 'Ho, for lots of adventures! Ho, for the answers to our questions,

in the end! WHOOPS! HIYAAAY! PEEP PEEP
PEEP!' Then she pressed a button, and her engine
sputtered to life. Lankin and Jeremy started up,
too, and in a very few moments they were in the air
again.

Chapter Three

The engine put-putted away. The balloon careened gently through a steely sky. Jeremy looked left. There was Bette, bobbing as she went. Jeremy looked right. There was Lankin, drawing back his bow, fitting in an arrow for another fray. Jeremy looked down.

There was Chegwith Skillett.

Chegwith Skillett was doing nothing. He was lying motionless, and staring at the sky, as usual.

'Isn't there anything that interests you at all?' said Jeremy.

'I don't believe so,' said Chegwith Skillett. There was a long silence.

'Cheggie,' said Jeremy.

'If I were disposed to do anything at all,' said Chegwith Skillett, 'I should beat you.'

'Well,' said Jeremy, 'at least it woke you up. Listen: I understand. I bet you think you're all alone. That you haven't got a single friend. Your father's dead. And even when he was alive, he wasn't really very kind to you. He let Humpidore have you. He didn't come to get you out. He didn't even come to see you very often. But you loved him all the same. You loved him very much.'

'Will you please shut up?' muttered Skillett, from the floor.

'But that doesn't mean you have to lose interest in everything,' said Jeremy, ignoring him. 'I mean, people go around all the time with questions in their minds. Haven't you got any? I have. Who's M'Graw, for instance?'

'I have no idea,' said Chegwith Skillett.

'He knew a lot about you and your father. How did he know all that?'

'I remain in the dark,' said Chegwith Skillett.

'There was something your father made that he wanted. He wanted it *really* badly, you know. What do you think it was?'

'I don't know,' said Chegwith Skillett, 'nor do I care. And you,' he added, 'are an inquisitive brat. There are many people like you who want to know more and more. But I am not of your kind. I want to know less and less. I wish to be a specimen of perfect ignorance.'

'*Crark parp hark shtarshkar harp harp shtarskar harp!*'

'The fact that I disagree with you,' said Chegwith Skillett, 'is no reason to abandon all attempts at clear communication.'

'It wasn't me,' said Jeremy. 'It was the radio. I don't think it's working properly. *Can't hear you!*' he bellowed into the mouthpiece.

36

'*Shtark!*' said the voice. '*Harppark derdark!*' Then, 'Is that better?' said Bette.

'Yes.'

'That's the trouble with anything Lankin rigs up. It's always likely to go on the blink. Now listen: we're heading north. It's going to get cold. I've put some jackets and helmets in your basket.'

'I can see them,' said Jeremy.

'Put them on now.'

They did. Or rather, Jeremy put on his own, and then did his best to put Chegwith Skillett's on Chegwith Skillett. It wasn't easy, since Skillett did nothing to help. Furthermore, Jeremy's jacket and helmet fitted just right. But Chegwith Skillett's were far too big. He lay there, in the end, staring at the sky and looking like a sort of discarded scarecrow pilot who can't be trusted even to frighten the birds. Jeremy stepped back and eyed him, despairingly; admired his own little outfit; then went to the side of the basket, and looked out.

Below was a barren, brown, unpeopled plain. After a while, it became a range of barren, brown, unpeopled hills. Then the hills became mountains, and bigger mountains. A huge, brown mountain loomed ahead, the biggest one of all.

'*Ssshark blark harp harp wark wark klaaark!*'

'It's on the blink again,' said Jeremy into the mouthpiece.

'That's where we're headed! The big one, I mean!'

Jeremy gazed at the great, hard slopes of jagged rock. 'That's where The Surveyor lives?' he cried.

'Yes. But where on the mountain, that's the point? There's an awful lot of mountain there.'

'I know where,' said Jeremy, and he pointed. Above them was a great, broad ledge of level rock. It hung above a chasm, and looked out over the foothills and the plain. 'That's the only place he could be!'

'Hm,' said Bette, 'I believe you're right.'

They manoeuvred carefully towards the ledge. There was room enough on it for a fleet of planes. Then a figure appeared. It was running towards them and waving frantically.

They landed, and Jeremy, Bette and Lankin got out. The figure came hurrying up. It was a man with wild, long, grey hair and bright eyes. He was wearing a brown smock, rough, brown leather leggings, and high, brown boots. He stopped when he saw them clearly, and looked intensely disappointed.

'Oh dear,' he said. 'No offence, but . . . I thought you were Chegwith Skillett, you see.'

'He's in there,' said Bette, pointing to the basket. The man went over and looked.

'Oh dear,' he said, coming back. 'No offence, but . . . he's *not*, you know. There's just some lunatic, lying on the floor.'

'He's the son,' said Jeremy. 'I expect it's the

father you wanted.'

'The *son?*'

'Yes,' said Bette.

'*That*'s the *son?*'

'Yes.'

'I didn't know there *was* a son.'

'There is. That's him.'

'Still less would I have thought he would have
been . . . like that.'

'Are you The Surveyor?'

'I am. And where is the real Chegwith Skillett,
then?'

'He's dead.'

The Surveyor staggered slightly. 'Dead?'

'Yes.'

For a moment, The Surveyor looked as though he were in great pain. He clung to Larry Lankin for support. Then 'How did he die?' he whispered.

'We thought you might know,' said Bette. 'Clearly, however, you do not.'

'Poor, poor Skillett,' whispered The Surveyor, sadly, and then, more sadly still, 'and what will become of my plans?'

'What plans?' said Bette. But The Surveyor was too unhappy to speak. After a time, he raised his head. 'Come to The Observatory,' he said.

There were just two buildings on the ledge – a little rock hut (which was where – he told them later – The Surveyor ate and slept) and a great big cube with lots of glass and a dome for a roof. It was there that The Surveyor led them now (with Chegwith Skillett on Lankin's back). As they went in, Jeremy gasped. The Observatory was full of telescopes: a great, fat, barrel one with a great, thick lens; a long, thin, tapered one, on stilts; one with an aerial, one with a screen, one that kept on printing facts and figures on a scroll; and one all knobs and buttons that grumped and buzzed and beeped. There were rows of smaller ones too.

'So,' said Jeremy, 'you're a stargazer.'

'By no means,' exclaimed The Surveyor.

'But you must be!'

'I am an *earth*gazer,' The Surveyor said. 'Let me explain. I think you ought to deposit your burden first.' Lankin laid Chegwith Skillett carefully on the floor. 'I have always dreamt of *knowing what things are about*.'

'Folly,' grunted a voice from the floor.

'What things?' asked Bette.

'The world. People. Things like that. I spent years down there, trying to know. Without success. But then I knew why I didn't know, if you know what I mean.'

'I'm lost,' said Bette.

'Me too,' said the voice from the floor. 'And always was,' it added, after a pause.

'I was too close to what I wanted to know. So I decided I'd have to be a long way off. I made some new equipment and I came up here.'

'And do you know now?' asked Bette.

'Sometimes I think I do,' said The Surveyor. 'And sometimes,' added The Surveyor, gloomily, 'I think I do not. Not the merest particle, in fact. That's why I needed my old friend Skillett. There are lots of inventors about, and some of us are really very great. But Skillett was the greatest of all. He was building a fabulous machine.'

'So that's what M'Graw was after,' breathed Jeremy.

'Skillett told no one exactly what it was. But I think *I know*.'

'What?'

'It was going to *explain*. To everyone. But first of all me, of course.'

'I don't believe it,' said Skillett, at once.

'I'm sure it was,' said The Surveyor. 'Everyone was going to know everything. And then we could all have had a rest.'

Suddenly, Bette looked worried. 'Listen!' she cried. A low heavy drone was coming from the air. Bette rushed over to a telescope, pointed it out of a window, and looked. 'I thought so!' she said. 'It's the Hookey Bandits!'

'Hookeys, ahaw!' echoed Lankin, and the two of them hurried to the door.

'Who?' said Jeremy, hurrying too.

'The Hookey Bandits,' said Bette, striding towards her plane. 'They're sky-raiders. Nasty, little, evil creatures. They bully, steal and spread trouble wherever they go. They're our especial enemies. They hate us and we hate them. In fact, they're our worst enemies. I bet they're here because they've noticed our planes.'

Jeremy could see them now. They were coming through the sky like a plague of little black bugs.

'We'll never make it!' Bette shouted to Lankin. She came to a halt. 'They're too close for us to escape, and there are too many of them to fight! We'd need Theresa and The Chunterer. Curses! Especially on Theresa!'

Bette was right. There were *a lot* of Bandits. So the four of them stood there (Chegwith Skillett was still on the floor) and waited.

One by one, the Hookey Bandits landed. Their planes were like little, black, tin torpedoes with an engine at the back and no wings. In each torpedo sat an ugly, grinning dwarf.

The largest dwarf had a shock of red hair. He sauntered up to Bette, and frowned. Then he grinned again.

'Eh eh!' he cackled. 'Whoops, eh? Whoops!'

The Bandits made their captives sit down. Then they tied their hands behind their backs. Then some of them went into The Observatory. There was a terrible bashing and smashing sound.

The Surveyor wept.

After a while, the Hookey Bandits came out of The Observatory. Four of them were carrying a human form.

'Reh eh eh!' they were cheering. 'Waaaaaaaah!' They threw Chegwith Skillett high in the air, caught him, and then swung him roughly from side to side.

They tied his hands behind his back, too. Then they led all five to the edge of the ledge. They took five long ropes, and hung their captives from the rock, so their feet were dangling over the chasm. They sawed halfway into the ropes, so the threads that were left started to fray slowly.

'Ray, ray!' howled the leader. 'Ichidee . . . ichiday . . . ichido . . . WHAAAAAAM!' The others all cheered and giggled like mad. The leader went over to Bette's rope, and Lankin's, and shook them a little. 'WHA-A-AM!' he crowed. 'WHA-A-AM! Byyyeee, goodies! Byyyeee! HRAAAH!' Then they all got back into their torpedoes. There was a blasting and a rattling and a roar of Bandit engines. The Bandits took off. Soon they were lost from view.

Jeremy's body suddenly shook. Another strand

44

had snapped in the rope. He stared below him. There was nothing for thousands of feet, and then just plain, hard rock. He felt very, very afraid.

'*Swine!*' screamed Bette. '*Vermin! Scum!* But I reserve my particular venom, anger, hatred and scorn for Theresa,' she added.

'So,' said The Surveyor, sadly, 'I shall fall to earth having never known. All those years of patiently gazing . . .'

'Were of course an utter waste of time,' said Chegwith Skillett, abruptly. 'But that was true in any case. I myself have four last words; simply: I take my leave.'

'You'd done that already,' said Jeremy. 'Taken leave of your senses, too.'

'You,' said Chegwith Skillett, 'are an insolent brat.'

Jeremy started to feel cheerful again. Then he felt more cheerful still. 'There's something on the horizon!' he yelled.

There was, as well; and it was coming towards them, fast. It came closer and closer. But Jeremy's cheerfulness didn't last long.

The approaching object was a white balloon.

A strand snapped, and another strand. The white balloon came floating up. It steered towards them, then hung in front. M'Graw and his cronies came forwards, and peered.

'Why, Surveyor!' said M'Graw, with a smile.

'Hello, M'Graw,' muttered The Surveyor, through clenched teeth.

'You two have met?' said Bette.

'We have indeed,' said M'Graw. 'How pleasant to see another of Skillett's old friends!'

'Don't pretend you were a friend!' cried The Surveyor. 'M'Graw,' he said, 'was Skillett's bitterest enemy. He's an inventor himself . . .'

'I am,' said M'Graw, preening a little. 'And a very great one, too. I am particularly proud of my Tracer and my Drill. The Tracer can track anything I tell it to (that's how I followed you, of course). And The Drill can pass through miles of the hardest rock in a few, paltry seconds.'

'But he knew that Skillett was greater than he. Far, far greater. So he was always trying to discover his secrets. Always trying to steal his plans. He envied him and he hated him.' M'Graw grinned. 'But he wanted Skillett's ideas. And most of all,' he shouted at M'Graw, 'you wanted his last and greatest idea: The Fabulous Machine . . .'

'Yes,' said M'Graw, with a laugh, 'I did. I intend to have it, too. I followed Skillett for years, trying to find it. But all in vain. Even The Tracer was of no avail. A cunning fellow was Skillett, oh yes. Now I rather admire the Hookeys (I know it was them who left you like this). They and I would make a fine team. I wouldn't want to spoil their handiwork. But I might, after all . . . if one of you tells me where Skillett's Machine is.'

'But Chegwith and I don't know!' shouted Jeremy. 'We've already told you that!'

'And I can't help you,' said Bette.

'And I don't know, either,' said The Surveyor, in despair.

'Are you all sure?' said M'Graw.

'Yes.'

'Because,' said M'Graw, 'if you're all *sure* . . . I think we must be on our way.'

'Aren't you going to save us?' said Bette.

'What would be my reason?' said M'Graw.

'Ordinary human kindness, I'd say.'

'I'm afraid I don't possess it,' drawled M'Graw.

'How about acting right, not wrong?'

'I have no interest whatever in that.'

'How about the sheen that comes of good deeds?'

'I'd rather the rust that comes of none.' Otto and Errol nodded their little, black caps. 'But I'm staying here talking for far too long. I must go in search of the Hookey Bandits. They're the very sort of allies of whom I shall have need. My friends, I must bid you farewell.'

'What are you going to do with the Machine if you find it?' shouted Jeremy. 'I'm sure Chegwith Skillett's father didn't mean it to do anything bad, you know. M'Graw, what are you planning to . . .' But the white balloon was receding fast. And

47

M'Graw had turned his back on them.

The sun was beating down. The strands were snapping fast. Jeremy's body began to twist.

The rope was on the point of giving way.

'I'm going to fall!' shouted Jeremy. 'It's ridiculous! I was playing in the garden, I saw a check bottom . . . and somehow I finished like this. I didn't know,' he added, 'that there could possibly be so much wickedness in the sky.'

'You may rest assured,' said Chegwith Skillett, 'that it is as nothing to the wickedness on earth. I, too, am about to fall. I came. I soared. I plummeted. The end.'

PHIIIING!

Chegwith Skillett disappeared.

PHIIIING!

The next moment, Jeremy found that he, too, was falling through empty air.

Chapter Four

He fell headlong past great stretches of crag. The wind hooted weirdly in his ears. The rocks below him came rushing up, sharply. His mind went blank with fright.

And then he hit something. And bounced.

Yes, he was bouncing. He went up in the air, hit the thing again, and bounced once more.

It was a net! He was bouncing in a net! And not far away was Chegwith Skillett, bouncing too!

There on either side were Theresa and The Chunterer, in their planes. They had the net between them, and were catching falling bodies as they went. They both looked across, and waved. Jeremy waved back.

Before very long, Lankin, The Surveyor and Bette had all been caught, too. Then the five of them clambered along the net and squeezed into the backs of the planes. Theresa and The Chunterer flew back to the plateau, and landed.

'You don't have to cheer,' said Theresa, holding up a hand as she clambered from her plane.

'Harrumph!' snorted Bette, glowering.

'We'd followed M'Graw from the start,' said Theresa.

'After you defied orders,' said Bette, still glowering.

'So we followed him here. Then we saw the Hookeys. We knew that something must be up. Then we saw M'Graw leave, too.'

'So rather than attacking at once,' said Bette, 'like the very *best* of daredevil pilots . . .'

'We looked through our telescope,' said Theresa, forbearingly, 'saw you hanging from the cliff, rigged up the net – that,' she said to Jeremy, 'being one of various pieces of equipment we always carry with us – and came in to catch you as you fell. Most of it was The Chunterer's idea, of course.'

'Thn thn hn thn,' said The Chunterer.

'So what now?' said Theresa, brightly, ignoring Bette's baleful glare. 'M'Graw and the Hookeys making a team. That doesn't bode well for us, you know.'

'Indeed,' said Lankin, 'ahaw!'

'They'll be up to no good. You can be sure of that.'

'We shall be equal to them,' said Bette, 'if we stay united. *United and together. At all times.*'

'The trouble is,' said Theresa, 'that it's hard to stay united with you. You're not really very uniting, you know. All the same, I'll try.'

'But where do we go now?' said Jeremy. 'Mr

Surveyor, this Machine. Where do you think it is?'

'If we can find it,' said Bette, 'maybe we can find out how Chegwith's father died.'

'We'd better find it quick,' said Jeremy. 'Before M'Graw and the Hookeys, in fact.'

The Surveyor was sitting on a rock and looking round him in despair. He raised his head slowly, and stared. Then, 'I think I know how Skillett died,' he said.

'But you didn't even know he was dead until we told you,' objected Jeremy.

'I know, all the same,' said The Surveyor. 'Skillett was obsessed with the Vanishing Point. He went there again and again. I expect he went one time too many, that's all.'

'Vanishing Point? What Vanishing Point?'

'The Vanishing Point,' The Surveyor explained, 'is an Air Zone far to the north. The air gets thinner and thinner there. And everything starts to change.'

'Everything?'

'Hm,' said Theresa. 'Would even Bette change, too?'

'Instruments, people, machines. The usual laws no longer apply. Everything behaves . . . unlike itself. Everything starts to go odd.'

'Bette,' remarked Theresa, 'is odd enough already.'

'At the Vanishing Point, nothing is the way

you'd expect. Everything starts to break up. The Vanishing Point is like a whirlpool, that's what Skillett used to say. It drags you in, slowly at first, when you're on the edge, then faster and faster and faster still . . .'

'It sounds exciting,' said Jeremy. 'But dangerous, too,' he added, with a frown.

'It is extremely dangerous,' said The Surveyor. 'To start with, there's time to stop and get out. But later . . . well, no one knows.'

'No one?'

'No one's been to the middle, you see. Even Skillett never went that far. But he wanted to. That's how I think he died. He went too far, in the end. That's where I think his Machine is, too.'

'In the Vanishing Point?'

'Not *in*, but *near*. Somewhere on the ground beneath. Skillett spent so much time there. It's the obvious place for the machine to be.'

'So,' said Bette, 'to the Vanishing Point we go.' There was a silence. 'I'm not quite sure,' added Bette, with a shiver, 'that we should really go very far . . . *into* the Vanishing Point, that is. It's sure to have awful effects on the planes.'

'I,' said Theresa, 'am a daredevil. A daredevil dares to do anything at all. Nonetheless – I – I think we might go *round*, not *in*. Round's good enough, to see if something's there.'

'Well,' said Jeremy, 'maybe all we'll need to do is

look at the ground beneath. How do we get there, Mr Surveyor?'

The Surveyor gave them directions. They all got ready to go. When they'd finished getting ready, 'Look,' said Bette.

Jeremy did. The net was still lying on the ground – and Chegwith Skillett was still on the net. He was lying there and staring at the sky. Jeremy and Bette went across.

'We must fold that away, I'm afraid,' said Bette.

'I have grown rather fond of this net,' said Chegwith Skillett. 'I very much enjoyed all that bouncing up and down. I can't think when I enjoyed myself more. Could you not tow me through the sky, in the net? Then I could bounce as I pleased.'

''Fraid not,' said Bette, tartly, starting to fold it up.

Slowly, lugubriously, Chegwith Skillett rolled to one side. 'The way of the world, no doubt,' he muttered. 'Of all the billion things to do, there is one – you discover – that is truly worthwhile. Then someone prevents the doing, forthwith.' At which point, Bette and Jeremy each grabbed one of Skillett's arms, and Lankin and The Chunterer each grabbed one of his feet, and between them they hoisted him back into the basket. Then they all prepared to take off.

The Surveyor was sitting on a rock, stock still,

and looking very, very miserable. Jeremy walked over to him.

'Come along,' he said. 'There's room in our balloon.'

The Surveyor sighed a very deep sigh. 'I did so want to know what things are about.'

'Well,' said Jeremy, 'let's find Skillett's Machine. Maybe it'll tell you, if it's what you think it is.'

'I could never use anyone else's machine. We inventors don't do that sort of thing. Not unless we're wicked, that is. I could make new instruments and start again. But it would take so long . . .'

'And you haven't really ever found out very much, anyway,' said Jeremy. 'Perhaps there are other ways of knowing things. Come with us, and maybe you'll see.'

The Surveyor gazed round. 'There is nothing left for me here,' he said. 'I accept your offer. Let's go.'

But after a while, back up in the air, Jeremy groaned.

For a time, he gazed down at the landscape below: cold, bleak, hilly, empty, with huge, dark forests and cold, dark, beautiful lakes. Then he looked round for company.

There was The Surveyor, sitting on the floor with his head in his hands, saying nothing; and there was Chegwith Skillett, lying on the floor and staring at the sky, and saying nothing either. And there was the radio hissing and crackling with a lot of *'parks'* and *'klarks'* and *'shtarskar harps'* that Jeremy couldn't understand at all.

It was all *very boring*.

Of course, Jeremy wasn't really bored. This was an adventure, after all, and a proper adventure, too. He would just have liked someone to talk to for a while. But since no one in the balloon was paying him any attention, he went through Skillett senior's possessions again. Walking-stick, flame-thrower, barrel-organ, plunger, key . . . Why, he wondered, had Skillett saved just these things? Were they to do with the Vanishing Point? They were clues to a puzzle that he didn't understand. What a strange man Skillett must have been. What strange things he must have been up to, too.

'Parp squark ssshark ssshark aark ntrark!'

'I can't hear you,' said Jeremy, wearily.

'There's smoke coming from your engine!' yelled Bette.

Jeremy ran to the edge of the basket and looked. It was true. The engine was smouldering. He ran back to the radio. 'What now?' he yelled.

'It's the same with anything Lankin rigs up. It's always likely to . . .'

'What now?'

By way of an answer, Bette waved at the ground. 'You'll have to take it down for Lankin to mend.

We'll follow you. Try to be as careful as you can. There are an awful lot of trees and water below.'

Jeremy gazed down, fearfully. Should he rouse The Surveyor and Skillett? But neither of them was going to be much help. He would have to do it all himself.

So, very gently, Jeremy let some air out of the balloon; and very gently, he steered his way down; and then he held his breath and scanned the ground. They floated over acres of pointy-looking firs, wobbled jerkily across a lake or two, and then reached a long, flat strip of shore. 'That'll do!' cried Jeremy – and sure enough, it did.

'Are we there?' said Chegwith Skillett, as though he'd just woken up.

'I'd forgotten all about you,' said Jeremy.

'I hadn't,' said Chegwith Skillett. 'Forgotten about me, that is. I try, but I can't. Are we there?'

'There where?'

'There where I was never interested in being.'

'I've made an emergency landing,' said Jeremy, proudly.

'You,' said Chegwith Skillett, 'are a clever brat.'

'There's something wrong with the engine. But here comes Lankin to fix it, now.' The planes were landing on the same strip of shore.

Lankin peered at the engine, and ahummed and ahawed for a very long time. And then he got out a lot of odd-looking tools, and started hacking and wrenching and twisting like mad. After a while, Lankin was covered in dirt and oil, but the engine was still in a great many pieces, and night was coming in, fast. Jeremy stared out across the lake. There was nothing to see but great, dark expanses of water and cloud and trees. They were very alone.

No they weren't.

A pair of fiery little eyes was watching them from the trees. Then another pair of eyes appeared, and another, and another. Jeremy stopped still and watched.

'Creatures,' breathed Bette, who'd seen them, too.

'What kind of creatures?'

'Are they going to attack?'

'They're getting closer.' They were. The darker it got, the closer they came. The flyers waited, silently.

'They're going to spring,' whispered Bette. Everyone grabbed something heavy and hard. 'We'd better strike first, before they do. Ready . . .'

'*No!*' roared a voice.

A figure came crashing through the trees and tramped out on to the shore. She was clutching a flaming torch.

It was a she, all right: a stout fat woman with wild black hair and a wild, strong face that was sort of jolly-sad. Her clothes were dirty, her boots were dirty, and her arms, face and hands were extremely dirty. She planted herself in front of the fliers, and frowned. Then 'A'right!' she shouted. 'Out now! Issafe!'

A funny little creature emerged from the forest, and stood there, waiting watchfully. Then a second emerged, and others, too. There were grey ones, brown ones and black ones; some big, some small and some middle-sized; some a bit like rabbits, some a bit like foxes, some like squirrels, some like little bears. They all had sharp, bright, inquisitive eyes, and they looked as though they could be fierce, if they tried.

'Name's Marta,' said the woman, warily.

'Are these your pets?' said Bette.

'*Pets!*' snorted Marta. 'Where *you* from?'

'We've come from the sky,' said Bette.

'Hah,' snorted Marta, as though that explained it.

'And I'm proud to be a member *of* . . .'

'Aeronauts Anonymous,' muttered the other three, feebly.

'They're tired,' said Bette. 'We've been mending an engine, but it's too dark now. Is there somewhere safe we can sleep?'

'There's me barn,' said Marta. 'If I let you, thaddis.'

'Oh, please do let us,' said Bette. 'We won't be any trouble. It's part of our code of honour, you know.'

So Marta took them to her barn, and showed them how to be comfortable; and then she made them a great, thick, vegetable hotpot; and then 'What are you doing here, all on your own?' asked Jeremy.

''S not,' snorted Marta. 'I's not on me own. Got me . . . *pets*,' and she snorted again.

'She's as bad as the Hookeys,' Theresa whispered.

''S not used 'em,' said Marta, who'd heard. ''S not used 'em for years. Words, that is. 'Cept with the flyers, now and then.'

'If your animals aren't pets,' said Jeremy, 'what

59

are they?'

'Me *cubs*,' said Marta. 'Family. Betterun pets, they are.'

'But they're not real family. Haven't you got a real family?'

'Shull tell yer?' said Marta.

'Preferably not,' sighed Chegwith Skillett. He was lying on the floor, swollen with vegetable hotpot, and staring at the ceiling.

'Shull tell yer? 'Bout me life?'

'No thank you,' said Skillett. Lankin swung out a warning boot. 'Very well,' said Skillett. 'I repent. If a story is the price of that *succulent* hotpot – for succulent indeed it was – then story we must have, to be sure.'

'I wuz very fond of someone,' said Marta. 'Dreamt of him, I did.'

'Oh dear,' said Chegwith Skillett. 'One of *those* stories. He wasn't fond of you, of course.'

'How d'yer know?' said Marta.

'People often aren't,' said Chegwith Skillett. 'Fond of each other, that is. No one, for instance, has been fond of me,' and he looked very melancholy. 'But yours is the usual tale. Girl meets boy, girl loves boy, boy scorns girl, et cetera. The other way round, from time to time. Is that the end of the story, now?' Lankin swung out a boot again. 'You should have given up, and let that be that.'

'Got sad, an' went. Wandered fer years. Ended

here, an' it was lovely an' quiet. S' I stayed for good.'

'But what about your creatures?'

'Got to know 'em. One by one. They wuz fond of me. I wuz fond of 'em. We all became family. That's it.'

'What did you mean about the flyers?' said Bette.

'Turn up here, every once in a while. Belv'dere Jones. Chegwith Sk'llett . . .'

'Chegwith Skillett!'

'Comes through here, every now an' agin.'

'Came,' corrected Bette.

'Nah,' said Marta. 'Comes. He'll be back.'

'What I mean is: Chegwith Skillett is dead.'

Marta looked incredulous. 'He's dead,' repeated Bette. Marta looked very upset. Her shoulders heaved. Her face went crinkly and old. 'You sure?' she whispered, at last.

'Belvedere Jones said so.'

'Pore old Skillett. *Pore* old Skillett.' Marta hugged herself. A great big tear went rolling down one cheek.

'How do you think he might have died?'

'Savin' a creature in trouble, I 'spect,' said Marta, mournfully. 'Wuz a kindly sort. Wuz making a great machine.'

'We know,' said The Surveyor.

'It wuz going to take care of unhappy things.' The Surveyor shook his head, in disbelief. 'Things as wuz hurt, and din' know what to do. Like all me

61

family, afore I took 'em in.'

'Do you know where Skillett's Machine is?'

Marta shrugged. 'Somewhere north, thassall,' she said.

Then Bette and Jeremy told Marta what they knew about Chegwith Skillett, and told her about M'Graw and the Hookey Bandits; and Marta told them the rest of the little she knew; and The Surveyor told Marta about his plans and his observatory, gloomily and at length. Jeremy introduced Marta to Chegwith Skillett junior. Marta – of course – could hardly believe her eyes.

Then Marta introduced them to all her little animals, one by one. And – though she sounded rough – she was so very good to her creatures, and so very kind to the flyers themselves, that they all decided that they liked her very much.

Finally, they went to the barn.

'One might get to know a great deal by observing animals,' muttered The Surveyor, as they all snuggled down for the night.

'Well,' said Jeremy, 'what I want to learn is at the Vanishing Point.'

'*Near* the Vanishing Point. I do not intend,' said Bette, 'that any of us should go *inside* the Vanishing Point.'

''N what Bette intends . . .' said Lankin.

'Is what no one does,' said a voice from the floor.

'Well,' said Bette, 'we'll see.'

Chapter Five

They did see, of course; because Lankin got up
early next morning, and fixed the engine before the
others were awake. Marta made them an *enormous*
breakfast, and then they all said their farewells.

'Except . . . ahem . . . for me,' said The Surveyor.

The others looked at him, inquiringly.

'You see,' said The Surveyor, 'I really have
nowhere to go. I do not wish to visit the Vanishing
Point. And I still want to know what things are
about. What better way – I have decided – than
observing – ahem – the creatures here.'

'But there are lots of better ways,' said Jeremy.

'So if you don't mind,' said The Surveyor to
Marta, ignoring him, 'I will build a little hut not far
away, and . . . ahem . . . observe.'

Marta frowned; looked suspicious; paced about;
but in the end said that she didn't mind; so long as
The Surveyor agreed to chop wood, fetch water,
clean her barn, sweep up dung, do the washing for
two and any other job that she didn't like herself.

The Surveyor said yes. The others said goodbye,
and went.

The air grew colder. The lakes below them were a chill, bright blue. The trees gave way to a vast wilderness of tawny moor. It seemed to stretch on endlessly, like nothing Jeremy had ever seen before. Here and there – in the marshier bits – it glinted with a million points of glittering, jewelled light.

'Chegwith?' said Jeremy.

'Hum,' said the voice from the floor.

'If you were interested in anything, I'd tell you to look at the ground. It's really amazing.'

'Hum,' said the voice, unimpressed.

'You really are very odd. You've spent most of your life in Humpidore's Home. I bet you've never seen much outside. But now you've *got* the chance, you ignore it all.'

'My dreams,' said Chegwith Skillett, 'are enough. I dream every night, you know.'

'Well,' said Jeremy, 'so do I.'

'But my dreams are entirely unique. Nobody else has dreams like mine.'

'How do you know?'

'My dreams are many-splendoured things.'

'Unlike the dreamer,' muttered Jeremy, looking at the scarecrow on the floor.

'They are rich, various and come in the most gorgeous colours. Dreams of travel, adventure, friends.' Chegwith Skillett sighed. 'After dreams like that, the real world palls.'

'Rubbish,' said Jeremy. 'What about Marta's vegetable hotpot? I bet that was better than a hotpot in your dreams.'

Chegwith Skillett looked sheepish. Then he licked his lips, furtively, and sighed. '*What* a hotpot,' he said.

'You ate twice as much as anyone else.'

'That vegetable hotpot,' said Chegwith Skillett, 'was a prodigy. Sheer bliss. One of the wonders of the world, I should submit, if I knew what the wonders of the world might be. That vegetable hotpot . . .'

'You see?' said Jeremy. 'I bet it was the same with the breakfast, too.'

Chegwith Skillett was forced to admit that it had been an extraordinarily good breakfast, and much more succulent than any dream breakfast could possibly be.

'Any *two* breakfasts,' said Jeremy. 'You ate The Surveyor's, as well. It's just the same with all the plain, ordinary things. You can't get the best ones in dreams at all.'

'About hotpots and breakfasts,' said Chegwith Skillett, 'you surely have a point,' and he sighed again.

'It's not just hotpots and breakfasts. It's anything your tummy tells you, or your eyes or your fingers or your tongue. OOOOOOF!'

All of a sudden, the balloon gave a crazy, little

up-and-down, zigzag lurch. Then it settled again.

'What was that?' whispered Jeremy.

'A hiccup in nature,' said Chegwith Skillett.

The balloon tipped a little to one side; tipped a
little to the other; then revolved several times, very
fast.

'A very large hiccup,' said Chegwith Skillett.
'More like an enormous belch, I'd say.'

'Skarskar warkar art art varp!'

The balloon sank swiftly; then went soaring up
again. Jeremy clung to the basket side.

'Ardar slarskar harp dedarp!'

He hauled his way round to the radio.

'I can't hear what you're saying!' he yelled.

The balloon went spinning off in one direction,
and then went spinning off in another.

'Clark! Itarp skittarp glark dedark!'

'What?'

'It's the Vanishing Point! We can't go any
further! Our planes won't survive it! And you're
too far in! Get out now, while you can!'

But it was already too late.

The balloon stopped spinning. It bounced a few
times, in a jolly way. Then it just held still.

And then the sky began to come apart.

Jeremy couldn't believe it. Patches – holes – were
appearing here and there; as though the sky had
been papered over another sky, and now the paper
was coming away. But holes were growing in the

second sky, too; and the third; and the fourth.

'Chegwith?' said Jeremy.

All at once, the sky sort of . . . flattened out.

'I . . . I think you ought to see *this*, you know.'

Forking paths appeared in the blue. The balloon seemed to be on every path.

'This isn't ordinary, Chegwith. It isn't a dream, either.'

Suddenly, Jeremy didn't know which path he was on. He didn't even know which balloon he was in. He was looking at himself from the second balloon, and looking at himself in the second from the third, and so on, and so on, and so on, and so on . . .

'Chegwith!'

The balloons were all going in different directions. So were the Jeremys, too.

'Chegwith! I'm scared! It's horrible! Help!'

Chegwith Skillett rose to his feet. In one of the balloons. In others he didn't. In others he rose, and then sank again. In one of the balloons, he held on to Jeremy's arm.

'That's me!' yelled Jeremy. '*Please* let that one – I mean this one – be me! I don't want any of the others. Take them away!'

'All right,' muttered Chegwith. 'I'll settle for this one myself, though I haven't the slightest clue as to why. Look,' he said, to Jeremy. 'Now we've decided which is us, the others appear to be fading away.' They were, too. In a few moments, there were no paths any more, and no extra balloons. The sky went back to normal again. 'How curious,' said Chegwith Skillett. 'What next, I wonder? What next, indeed.'

Jeremy shivered, fearfully; sank to the floor; and crouched there in a huddle for a while. Chegwith Skillett marched round the basket, several times, very fast, like a mad sentry on duty. Every time he reached a corner, he halted, peered then sang out, 'All's well here!'

'Can we start going back?' said Jeremy, at last.

'No,' said Chegwith Skillett, 'I'm afraid we can't,' and he pointed, grimly. 'All's not as well as I thought.'

Jeremy struggled to his feet, and stared. The sky had frozen in place.

It was hard, huge, empty; like a great vast chamber of solid blue, with granite-looking clouds immobile in space. The balloon was held fast, too. Even the smallest sound echoed and echoed and echoed away.

'Behold our fate,' whispered Chegwith Skillett. 'We made a choice. We stuck to it. Now – it would seem – we are stuck ourselves.'

'I'm starting to feel stuck, too,' said Jeremy, slowly.

'What do you mean?'

'I can hardly move. Or . . . think. Or . . . speak.'

'Me too,' said Chegwith Skillett. 'But we must
. . . fight back, don't you think?'

Jeremy was silent.

'You,' said Chegwith Skillett, 'are a frozen brat.'

Jeremy did not respond.

'One of us must make . . . great efforts,' said
Chegwith Skillett, after a while.

Jeremy said nothing.

'Then it will have to be . . . me,' said Chegwith
Skillett.

Languidly, heavily, silently, a single, large,
white bird came winging out of the distance
towards them. It glided up to them, staring
unseeing, then glided past, and away.

'Is there something behind all this?' shouted Chegwith Skillett.

'Behind all this,' said the echo.

'I do not care,' shouted Skillett, 'whether there is anything behind all this or not! I think it is time we were freed!'

'Time,' called the echo. 'Time,' it sang.

'And you,' shouted Chegwith Skillett, 'can shut up!'

'Up,' said the echo, mockingly. 'Up.'

'Release our balloon!' roared Chegwith Skillett.

'Loon!' sang the echo, gleefully. 'Loon!'

'Don't be so insulting,' said Skillett. 'I am not.' All at once, he got angry. He raised his hands, laboriously, and shook the sides of the basket, very hard. 'I'll show you!' he cried. He began to gabble, very fast indeed. The most extraordinary gibberish came bubbling up from his throat. The echo tried to keep up. But it couldn't. Before very long, the whole, great, frozen sky was ringing and singing with a buzz and a babble and a huge confusion of sound.

It was all too much for the sky. The sky cracked. Little crevices went wriggling across it here, there and everywhere. They joined, divided, joined, divided in a crazy lattice of lines. The sky was a patchwork now. And the patches were coming away again; flaking off in sheets, like plaster from ceilings or walls. And this time there was nothing beyond them at all.

A wind came hooting and howling from the holes.

It hooted and whistled and whirled and swirled and it swept the balloon up and away and along in a surging, howling hurricane of air.

Somewhere, Skillett found a rope. Somehow, he roped them both to the side. It was then that the shapes began to appear.

First of all, it was just balloons; lots and lots of little, faded balloons; as though the Vanishing Point had become a sort of graveyard for every balloon that had ever floated away from a child. Then there were the birds: different flocks of colourless birds flapping very slowly over, round and past the balloon.

'You know how photographs have negatives?' whispered Chegwith Skillett.

'Yes,' whispered Jeremy.

'Well, I've no idea myself,' said Chegwith Skillett, 'but someone told me about it once. This is like the negative of the sky. Of the sky we normally see, that is.'

After the birds came the flyers: hundreds of flyers, in every sort of craft. They roared and chugged and glided by, white-faced, upright, completely still, gaping straight ahead of them. But it was what came last that was worst of all.

It was like a giant float, or an airborne open cart.

It was white, and there were lots of tall, gaunt, white-clad people on it. Some of them were moaning, faintly. Others leered and beckoned as they went. Some of them just stared, hollow-eyed.

In the middle of them all was a small, worm-like thing. It had a face. The face was grinning, horribly.

Then Jeremy saw a balloon hurrying towards them. It was a large, black, sinister balloon. It came from one corner of the sky, but in a very few moments it had blotted out the float, the worm, the people, everything. It loomed hugely over their own balloon like a monstrous cloud above a tiny fishing boat. The sky entirely vanished from view. The black balloon took hold of theirs and started to tow it away, very fast.

'It's the end!' screamed Jeremy, as they raced along. 'I'd rather the Hookeys! At least, you knew who they *were*!'

'Do not fear!' shouted Chegwith Skillett, and he planted himself firmly on his feet, folded his arms, and frowned, grandly.

'What are you *doing*?' yelled Jeremy.

'I intend to brave the worst!' roared Skillett. 'On both our behalfs! I intend,' he roared, 'to become *the Napoleon of Balloonists*!' The balloon pitched wildly. Napoleon Skillett crashed to the floor. 'I shall not be daunted!' he bellowed, scrambling to the side. '*Down*, black terror, but by no means *out*!' and he levered himself to his feet.

72

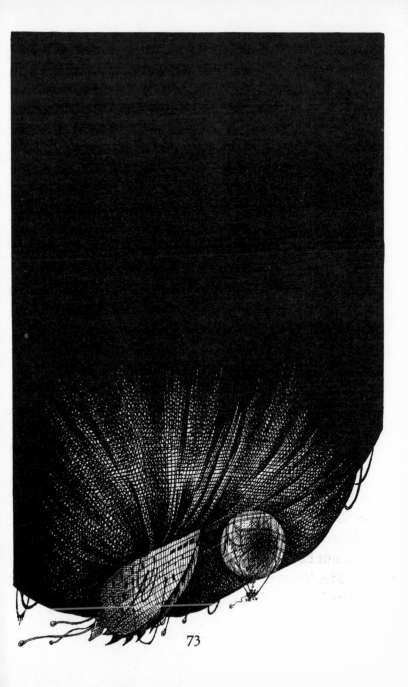

Jeremy was on his feet, too. 'Chegwith,' he shouted, 'look!' Chegwith Skillett looked. 'It's towing us *away from the Vanishing Point*!'

It was, too. The balloons were back above the lakes and the moor. And not only that: the black balloon was slowing down. It was shrinking and changing colour, as well. Before very long, it looked hardly any bigger than their own. The black had turned to a bright sky blue.

'I confess to being baffled,' mumbled Chegwith Skillett.

The blue balloon moved lazily over the moor. There was a vast, bleak sea ahead. The blue balloon descended to the shore, pulling the other as it went.

They landed with a bump. The blue balloon was some way away. Jeremy gazed at the basket. He could see the figure of a man.

'Who is it?' he said.

'I do not know.'

'Chegwith,' said Jeremy, shuddering, 'I feel even more scared than I did before. I don't know why, but I do.'

'We Napoleons of the sky,' said Chegwith Skillett, 'are not to be scared by a single man.'

'Are you *sure* you feel like Napoleon?' said Jeremy. Napoleon nodded. 'Well, you'd better not go back to the way you were. He's coming towards us. Now.'

Chapter Six

The man strode steadily towards them. He was a tall, handsome, distinguished-looking man in a dark flying suit and a crimson cloak. He wore white gloves, carried a cane in one hand, and he was smiling.

All of a sudden, Chegwith Skillett gave a cry.

'Napoleons don't make noises like that,' said Jeremy, crossly.

'We're safe, boy, safe! *It's Belvedere Jones!*'

The man came up to Chegwith Skillett. 'Young Chegwith,' he said, 'I thought as much.' Chegwith introduced him to Jeremy. 'I assume you are unhurt?' said Belvedere Jones.

'Unscathed,' said Chegwith Skillett, 'and unbowed,' and he frowned his Napoleon frown.

'How do you feel? The Vanishing Point can have dreadful effects.'

'We are in the best of spirits,' said Chegwith Skillett, grandly.

'Speak for yourself,' said Jeremy. 'It was horrible. I hated it.'

'You were too far in. For novices, at least. To learn how to navigate the Point takes years. Even then, one knows only a part.'

'Anyway,' said Jeremy, 'thank you for saving us.'

'Pleased to be of service. I happened to be there myself – I often am, it is a favourite spot – and I recognized the balloon. It had to be you, of course.'

'It didn't have to be *me*,' said Jeremy. 'I wish it hadn't been, too.'

'But how do you come to be here?' said Belvedere Jones, to Chegwith Skillett.

'We decided . . .' said Chegwith Skillett.

'*We*?' said Jeremy.

'To try to find out how my father died.'

'To try to find his Machine, as well.'

'Ah yes,' said Belvedere Jones, rather vaguely. 'I believe he told me about some machine.'

'What was it for? Do you know?'

'I really took very little interest. It was meant to grant one a great deal of power. That's what Skillett said, if I remember rightly.'

There was a pause. Then, 'You never told me how he died,' said Chegwith Skillett, softly.

'I'm afraid I don't know,' said Belvedere Jones.

'Then how do you know he's dead?'

Belvedere Jones looked grieved. There was a tiny twitch at the corner of his mouth. He wandered sadly to a rock by the sea, and sat down on it. The others sat down on either side.

'Your father . . . just vanished,' said Belvedere Jones. 'We – his friends – lost touch with him. To start with, we thought nothing of it.'

'*Thought nothing of it?* Why?'

'Your father had a hideaway, known only to himself. We simply thought he'd gone there. He often did, you know.'

'Perhaps he did this time,' said Chegwith Skillett. 'Perhaps he's still in his hideaway, too.'

But Belvedere Jones shook his head. 'It has been too long. After a time, he always came back. This time he hasn't. He can only be dead.'

They stared at the cold, blue sea. It looked as though it might stretch to the very ends of the world. After a while, Chegwith Skillett gave a long-drawn-out, melancholy sigh. Then he hung his head, quietly, and wept.

'Poor, sad Napoleon,' said Jeremy, and he hugged Chegwith Skillett, as hard as he could.

Skillett looked up. There were tears in his eyes. 'Perhaps he died in the Vanishing Point,' he said.

Belvedere Jones shook his head. 'He knew it too well to let it beat him. No. I would guess it was . . . M'Graw.'

'M'Graw who killed him?'

'The same,' said Jones. 'Have you met M'Graw?'

'He tried to kill us,' said Jeremy.

'He hated Skillett more than anything else.'

Chegwith Skillett brushed away the tears, and stood up. Then he paced around the rock, several times, snapping his fingers. 'We must find the Machine!' he cried.

'Chegwith,' said Jeremy, suddenly.

'My boy.'

'I think I'd like to go home.'

'Home? To the Bartholomews?'

'Not to them. But to my parents, yes. Your father's dead. You can't change that.'

'You,' said Chegwith Skillett, 'are a timorous brat. But I can find my father's Machine before M'Graw,' he went on, sitting down again. 'I can thwart that villain!' he roared, rising and pacing round the rock. 'I can turn the tables on the murderer!' he cried, hopping about in a rage. 'At least . . . I can *try*,' and he sat down again.

'But no one knows where the Machine is. No one ever did, apart from your Dad.'

'I think Chegwith is right,' said Jones. 'I also think that *he is the very person* to find the Machine.'

'The very person!' cried Jeremy, in disgust. 'He doesn't know anything! He doesn't want to know anything! He wants to be a specimen of perfect ignorance!'

''That was before I became the Napoleon of Balloonists,' objected Chegwith Skillett.

' "My son is my heir in everything." That's what your father once said to me. Which must have meant the Machine, as well. Not that I care, myself. The loss of Skillett is beyond repair. But something he gave you. Something he said . . .'

Chegwith Skillett paced round and round the rock. He rummaged in his straw-coloured hair. He pulled pleadingly at his ears. 'Can't recall a thing,' he said, at last. 'Nonetheless, I am firm. I shall find that Machine, or bust. And I hereby vow,' he added, to Jeremy, 'that as soon as I have found it, I shall return you to the world of the Humpidores. And welcome to it you shall be.'

'Right,' said Belvedere Jones. 'But now you've decided, don't give up. That's what your father would have said.'

'I shall persist!' boomed Chegwith Skillett. 'I shall prove firm of purpose! Indomitable! I shall persevere to the very end! I shall wing to my goal as the arrow to the target! I . . .'

'I must be going,' said Belvedere Jones.

'You aren't coming with us?'

'Alas, I can't. But we will meet again, and before too long.'

Belvedere Jones shook hands with them both, then strode to his balloon, and cast off.

Chegwith Skillett took one last look at the sea. It was empty. Not a bird, not a boat, not a single sign of life.

'Poor old Dad,' he whispered. Then he flourished his fists in the air, very fiercely. 'Vengeance,' he cried, 'shall be mine!'

'*Ours*,' said Jeremy. 'Remember me?'

'Vaguely,' said Skillett, stalking hurriedly back to the balloon.

'You wouldn't be here if I hadn't helped.'

'Be that as it may, I am all here now. I am in fact extremely here. I am so very here that I want to leave here and head off there, if you see what I mean.'

'I'll tell you what I can see,' said Jeremy.

'Be brief,' said Chegwith Skillett. He was in the basket, and casting off.

'I can see you're as mad as ever. In a different

way, that's all.'

'Then you will hardly need more of my company,' said Chegwith Skillett. The balloon rose from the ground.

'Stop!' yelled Jeremy, diving at the basket side, and clinging on. They continued upwards, Jeremy wailing and kicking his feet.

Chegwith Skillett peered down at him. 'You are heading in the wrong direction,' he remarked. 'I thought you wanted to go back home.'

'Help me!'

'I wouldn't stay there for very long, if I were you. The Bartholomews . . .'

'Damn the Bartholomews!'

'I'll pretend I didn't hear that,' said Chegwith Skillett.

'Pull me up!'

Reluctantly, Skillett did.

They headed back where they'd come from, looking for Aeronauts Anonymous. They were careful to avoid the Vanishing Point.

They journeyed on for some time. Then Jeremy pointed. 'What's that?' he cried. A cloud of black smoke was spreading across the sky.

'I do not know,' said Chegwith Skillett, knotting his brows and pinching his nose. 'But I can't say I like it. I smell foul play,' and he set the balloon on course for the smoke.

It was foul play, all right. The smoke was coming

from Belvedere Jones's balloon. A dozen Hookey Bandits were on the attack. M'Graw was watching, nearby.

'RAY!' yelled the Hookey Bandits. 'RAY RAY! RAAAAH! Byeee, goody! Bye bye byeeee!'

Belvedere Jones had a pistol, and was firing as best he could. But he'd been surprised, and was quite outgunned. His balloon was rapidly losing height.

'*Crew!*' yelled Chegwith Skillett. '*Man the guns!*'

'Er . . . we haven't got any guns,' said Jeremy.

'Oh very *well* then,' said Chegwith Skillett, peevishly. 'Stand by whatever you've got.'

'I haven't got anything at all,' said Jeremy. 'A key, a blowlamp, a walking-stick . . .'

'*Forget it,*' growled Skillett. '*Chaaaarrrge!*'

'I don't think we should,' said Jeremy.

'*Traitor!*' bawled Skillett. '*Craven cur! Chicken-hearted yellowbelly! Little baby bunting! Cowardy, cowardy, shamefully cowardy custard!*'

Jeremy pointed up above them. It was Aeronauts Anonymous. They were chugging down on the Hookeys. They had the sun behind them, and were ready for the fray.

'Right!' shouted Skillett. 'We'll get M'Graw!'

'I think we'd better rescue Belvedere Jones,' said Jeremy, and he pointed. The blue balloon was hurtling downwards. It looked as though it were out of control.

'Hm,' said Chegwith Skillett. 'I believe you're right.'

So they started off down in pursuit. But the blue balloon was sinking fast – faster than they could go themselves.

'It's curtains, I'm afraid,' said Chegwith Skillett, and he stood to attention, solemnly. 'A good man down. Fire the salute.'

'We haven't got anything to fire with,' said Jeremy. 'Anyway, it's not curtains at all,' and he waved. The Chunterer's plane went clattering and wheezing by.

'Ahah,' said Chegwith Skillett, stroking his chin. 'Let us hope the lad is up to the job.'

The Chunterer was, of course. He spun a lasso round his head, roped Jones's motor with a single throw, then pulled the blue balloon down to the ground. The others followed them, and landed, too.

Belvedere Jones got out of his basket, flicked a glove at some dirt on his cloak, and went over to The Chunterer. 'A superbly conducted rescue,' he said. 'My respects – and my thanks, of course.'

'Hn thn thn hn thn,' said The Chunterer.

Bette, Theresa and Lankin landed, too. M'Graw and the Hookeys had been driven off. Skillett introduced the Aeronauts to Belvedere Jones. Then 'Have you noticed where we are?' said Bette. Jeremy looked round. They were back by the lake where Marta lived. 'That was The Chunterer's idea:

to land in a place which we knew was safe. The Chunterer is a very wise man. When we're in trouble . . .'

'It's The Chunterer who turns up trumps.'

'As I may have said before,' said Bette. 'I suggest we now repair to Marta's.' Chegwith Skillett nodded, vigorously. '*To rest*,' said Bette, 'not to eat. Then we mend Mr Jones's balloon. And then we go on our way.'

So they walked to Marta's. They went very quickly, with Chegwith Skillett leading the way. But Marta wasn't there. Nor were her creatures. Nor was The Surveyor. Skillett looked very disappointed. He searched every corner of the house; the kitchen, in particular. But there was no one around.

So they trudged their way back to the planes, with Chegwith Skillett bringing up the rear. And then, when they were nearly there, 'Oh no!' gasped Bette.

The planes and the balloons had all been wrecked. Wings had been staved in. Engines had been smashed. The baskets had been broken. The balloons had been let down. There was wood, glass and metal all around.

M'Graw emerged from the trees. So did Otto and Errol. A dozen Hookeys came out, too. They all had weapons, and were pointing them.

'COOOO!' said the leader of the Hookeys. 'Poor

ole goodies! Hee hee hee!'

M'Graw smiled, too. 'It was easier to wait till you were on the ground,' he said. 'Now, what shall we do with you? First things first,' and he turned to Belvedere Jones. They stared at each other, levelly.

'It has been a long time, Jones,' said M'Graw.

'It has indeed,' said Belvedere Jones.

'You are the real threat, of course.'

'To you, I would be, yes.'

'Whatever else, you must be . . . expunged.'

The Hookeys giggled, cheered and raised their weapons. Otto and Errol guffawed.

And then there was a rustling and pattering and a snorting and a barking and a roaring in the woods. M'Graw spun round. The Hookey Bandits gaped. Hordes of creatures came scuttling out and launched themselves at their foe. A little ball of fur sprang straight at M'Graw's face, and clung to it, howling with glee. M'Graw tore it away and bawled for help. Then a shaggy goat came up from behind and butted M'Graw, again and again. A herd of small, wild hogs toppled Otto and Errol to the floor. Bands of racoons and sloths and squirrels came dropping from the trees on the Hookey Bandits' heads.

It was a rout.

M'Graw fled yelling with the goat still at his rear. Otto and Errol fled, too, with Chegwith Skillett after them, brandishing a stick. The Hookey

Bandits scattered blindly in all directions, howling.

The noise died away in the distance, and Marta came out of the trees. She looked very pleased with herself. She went round patting all the creatures.

''Em's not fierce,' she said. ''Em's gentle things. Harmless, like. But if I tell 'em, they'll fight.'

'Well,' said Bette, 'we're very glad you did. Tell them, that is. Aren't we, Mr Jones?'

'Indeed,' said Belvedere Jones. His hair was still perfectly in place. His cloak, suit and gloves were spotless and uncreased. He was as calm and debonair as before. Danger seemed not to disturb him in the least.

'He's the *real* ace,' said Jeremy, in awe.

Bette had been talking to Marta. 'We're agreed!' she shouted. 'We'll stay here until the planes and balloons are mended. If that's all right with you, Mr Jones,' she added, in a respectful tone. Belvedere Jones nodded. 'Then we'll decide on what to do next.'

'Where's Chegwith?' said Jeremy. Chegwith Skillett had not returned.

'I should never have let him go,' said Jeremy, after a pause. 'He might do anything at all. And anything might happen to him.'

They waited, anxiously. After a while they started to call.

'Supposing he's been kidnapped,' said Bette. 'That's just the advantage M'Graw would want.'

Theresa snorted. 'No one,' she said, 'could want an advantage like that. That's not what "advantage" means.'

Then Chegwith Skillett appeared. He was covered in mud, rotten leaves and berry stains, and he was grinning broadly and panting hard. He looked red and joyous. In one hand he held two little black caps. He threw them to the ground, sat down and gasped for breath.

'*The spoils of war!*' he rumbled, at last.

'And Otto and Errol?'

'I left them prostrate beneath a tree.'

'*Very* prostrate?'

'They were *exceedingly* prostrate, yes.' Chegwith Skillett stood up, thrust back his shoulders and banged his chest. Then he did *hundreds* of press-ups. Then he jogged around the clearing, by way of showing that he felt quite hale. Lastly, he went up to Marta.

'The hero has a request,' he said.

'Whassat?'

'The hero of the battlefield, man among men . . .'

'What men?'

'The hounder of the foe, great bearer of the banner . . .'

'You got no banner.'

'The gleaner of trophies has a single plea.'

'Whaddissit, galoot?'

'Let's eat.'

So they did.

Chapter Seven

When they'd finished eating; when Chegwith
Skillett was sitting there with a swollen stomach,
and a silly grin on his face:

'So,' said Bette, 'we're still none the wiser.'

'I am,' said Chegwith Skillett.

'You are *not*,' said Theresa, firmly. 'You're a
nutter, just like before.'

'I have braved the Vanishing Point,' said Skillett,
proudly.

'That wasn't wise,' said Theresa.

'But it *made* me wise. Very wise. So wise, in fact,
that you ought to do just what I say.'

Bette took a deep breath. 'I *meant*,' she said, 'that
we still can't be sure where the Machine is, or how
your father died.'

'That's beside the point,' said Theresa. 'We've
got no planes to reach it in.'

'Cud walk,' said Marta, suddenly.

'Walk?' said Theresa.

'Sk'llett walked.'

'In this great, big, wild, empty forest . . .'

'*Skillett?*' said Bette.

''Walked, ivry now and agin.'

The others all looked at her, inquiringly.

'The weather. 'S sometimes bad for days. If it wuz bad, then Sk'llett walked. Allers took 'sem path.'

'Which path?'

'The naaaarsty one. *Wickid*, it is. 'Ud never use it, meself. But Sk'llett wuz so keen to git there, yussee.'

'Get where?' said Chegwith Skillett, sitting bolt upright.

'Git where he wuz gitting, galoot.'

'In other words, the Machine!' said Chegwith Skillett, springing from his chair in a single bound. 'I'll bet,' he declared, striding frantically from wall to wall, 'that this is where we shall find the Machine! At the end of this so-called "wickid" path.' He lunged at Jeremy and grabbed an arm. 'We must depart,' he said. 'At once. Forthwith. Post-haste.'

'But it's *wickid*,' said Marta. 'There's 'orrible things there. I *dunno* what.'

'My father must have survived it,' said Chegwith Skillett. Marta nodded. 'Well so – I believe – can I. I shall rely on my sheer doughtiness.'

'Your what?'' said Jeremy.

'Doughtiness.'

'What's that?''

'It is the stuff,' said Chegwith Skillett, 'of which

warrior heroes and Napoleons are made.'

'Ah. *That* stuff.'

'Yes.'

'Being funny in the head.'

'If I were disposed to pause for a while,' said Chegwith Skillett, 'I should thrash you.' Belvedere Jones got to his feet. Everybody except Chegwith Skillett went quiet. Chegwith Skillett went on rushing noisily from wall to wall.

'Chegwith,' said Jones, 'this is not a good idea.'

'The rushing?' said Skillett, still rushing.

'The path,' said Jones. 'It will shortly be night. Wait until everything is mended. Then we will follow the path from above.'

'We?'

'Yes. We.' The others all grinned, and looked very pleased.

'I had the impression,' said Chegwith Skillett, 'that you weren't interested in my father's Machine.'

'That is the case. But I'm interested in you.'

'In other words, you wish me to be patient.'

'Yes.'

'Collected.'

'That is so.'

'Quietly determined.'

'Exactly.'

Chegwith Skillett stopped and looked round. Little by little, he lowered his head.

And then he did a big leap in the air. 'Well,' he roared, 'I shan't! *Whoops whoops yippee! Let's go, boy, go!*'

So he and Jeremy went stalking back to the balloon, took out everything they needed, and packed. They also packed the items of junk. Then Skillett grabbed the peculiar walking-stick.

'Now I know what this was for!' he yelled. 'Skillett (the younger) follows in father's footsteps. Skillett (the younger) takes possession of father's stick!'

Bette sidled up to Jeremy. '*You* don't have to go, you know,' she whispered. Jeremy nodded. 'Aren't you afraid?' Jeremy nodded, again.

'But someone's got to help him if he gets into trouble,' he said.

'Well, keep to the path whatever you do. We'll all come looking just as soon as we can.'

'*Boy!*' boomed Skillett. '*Let us sally forth!*' And off they went.

The path wound narrowly through sombre trees. It was silent, and full of shadows.

'Chegwith,' said Jeremy, nervously, 'let's go back.'

Chegwith Skillett was charging ahead, chopping at plants with the walking-stick. 'I refuse!' he hollered, gaily. 'Sorry, old man!'

'We don't know where this leads or what's

ahead. It's lonely and dark, and it's getting darker, too. We're sure to get lost. Then that will be that.'

Chegwith Skillett shook his head. 'M'Graw must be thwarted, don't you agree?'

'Well, yes . . .'

'His evil must not prosper. Is that not so?'

'Of course. But . . .'

'Then someone has to make sure of it. Saying must be doing, from time to time.' He took a great swipe at a plant.

'But Chegwith, not long ago, you weren't doing anything at all.'

'That – ahem – was in another life.'

'Actually,' said Jeremy, 'it was this morning.'

'This morning,' said Skillett. 'An *age* ago. There's no way back, now. Forward, boy. *Forward!*' and he plunged along the path, whirling his stick at the looming trees.

They clambered over rotten trunks, and scuffed their way through needles and cones. They brushed cobwebs from their faces, and waved off crowding motes of dust. Here, there and everywhere there were great dark avenues that led away to nothing at all. No one had ever gone down them. No one ever would. How gloomy, Jeremy thought to himself; or rather, how gloomy it might have seemed, had it not been for his friend. For Skillett was quite unabashed. He chattered. He chanted. He hooted. He laughed. Sometimes he let out a cry, and scuttled to a nest of scarlet toadstools, or a rich little glow of golden mould.

But after a while, even Skillett went quiet. It was damp. It was cold. They were hungry and tired. The trees seemed unending. The night was black.

'*But . . .*' said Skillett.

'But what?'

'My father could not have walked so *very* far without finding somewhere to rest. We shall hit on it soon. You mark my words.'

Sure enough, the forest divided in two, and ran across two lines of hills. Between the hills was a mist-strewn valley. And in the middle of the valley was a house; or better, a mansion; or even better, a hall. It was a huge disjointed pile of stone with jutting lumps here and a slewed wing there and a scatter of chimneys all over the roof. In front of it stood a still black pond. There were lots of lightless windows, and an old, black, wooden door.

They went to the door, and knocked. No one appeared.

'Since no one wishes to come out,' said Skillett, 'I shall now go in.'

'Oh dear,' said Jeremy.

Skillett tried the door. It opened with a long, slow croak. 'Hulloa!' bellowed Skillett. 'Is anybody there?'

There wasn't; not that they could see. They were in a huge hallway, with stairs ahead – and what a

hallway it was.

It was simply a ruin. There were holes in the
floor. The walls were giving way. The stairway was
rotten, the banisters were down, and dust and
plaster were everywhere. There were beams
against walls and lying on the floor, where the
ceiling had partly collapsed. A few brown
tapestries hung damply down, and a heavy
wooden chair stood awkwardly near by. Two
smoking torches cast a little dull light. Otherwise,
the place was bare.

'Hulloa!' shouted Chegwith Skillett, again. A
large patch of plaster thudded softly on the floor.
Skillett went quiet.

In the shadows on the stairs, something moved; something large, misshapen, clumsy, strange. Chegwith Skillett ran to the torches, and hoisted one in the air.

It was a man; a . . . sort of man. He had an extremely large head, a big, lumpy body, and an amazingly sad and ugly face. He looked at them both, in silence.

After a while, 'I am Tarkus,' he said. He gave a long, low groan.

'Well, Tarkus,' said Skillett, 'this isn't much of a welcome, you know.'

'You are welcome to it all,' said Tarkus, groaning again.

'Thanks,' said Chegwith Skillett. 'But we . . . er . . . have no need. You can keep it all to yourself.'

'There is nothing here,' said Tarkus, as though it needed pointing out. His great, gloomy head went wagging from side to side. 'Nothing for anyone. Least of all me.'

'Well,' said Skillett, 'that depends. You never can tell with nothings. You may *think* they're nothing. But others may not. Nothings can turn into somethings, too. For instance: have you ever heard of Chegwith Skillett?'

Tarkus looked astounded. 'Yes,' he whispered. 'I have, indeed.' He pondered for a while. Then, 'Do you know him, too?'

'I,' said Skillett, 'am his son.'

'Oh,' said Tarkus. 'A son?' He paused again, and thought. 'I used to see him often. Your father, that is. But not for a long time, now,' and Tarkus looked very troubled.

'I'm afraid,' said Skillett, 'that my father is dead.'

Tarkus looked distraught. He stared and stared. Then, slowly, his great head sank.

'Then all hope is lost,' he mumbled, at last.

'Far from it,' said Skillett. 'Jeremy and I are hoping to follow in his tracks. There are others who are hoping to join us, too. Some of them are hoping . . .'

'I meant,' said Tarkus, 'for *me*.'

'Ah,' said Skillett, 'of course. But why?'

'Your father – you see – was making a Machine.'

'We know,' said Jeremy.

'In that case,' said Tarkus, 'you will have heard of me.'

"Fraid not,' said Skillett, briskly. 'No offence, of course.'

'But you must,' said Tarkus. 'The Machine was for me.'

'That's what everyone says,' said Jeremy.

'What "everyone"?' asked Tarkus, suspiciously.

'The usual sort,' said Skillett. 'All of them. That is: the lot.'

'Everyone who talks about the Machine.'

'There is no "everyone",' said Tarkus. 'Just me.'

'I'm afraid there are others, as well. My father's numerous friends, in fact. And they all say exactly the same. Exactly different, of course, as well, if you see what I mean.'

'No,' said Tarkus. 'His friends?' Chegwith Skillett nodded. 'But *I* was his friend.'

'Er . . . people do have more than one friend,' said Skillett. 'Not myself, that is,' he mumbled, looking down. 'In my case, no friends at all. But it has been known to happen, from time to time, in this outrageously confusing world of ours.'

'Well,' said Tarkus, 'I was the real one. I was the one your father was going to help.'

'How was my father going to help you?'

'The Machine was going to make me happy, at last.'

'I see,' said Chegwith Skillett. 'My father was building an amazing Machine to make you, Tarkus, happy.'

Tarkus nodded. 'I am miserable, you see.'

'Then that explains it,' said Skillett.

'I have always been miserable. *Terribly, terribly* miserable. The house. The trees. The sky. The wind. The rain. The snow, when it comes. The Hordes from The City, of course. They all make me miserable. But Skillett told me he could change all that.'

'Well,' said Chegwith Skillett, 'talking of misery: you can help us out of ours, right now.'

'Are *you* miserable, too?' said Tarkus, wonderingly.

'Sort of,' said Skillett. 'We've come a long way. We need rest for the night. We're . . . hungry, too.'

'Food,' said Tarkus, musingly. He scratched his head. 'I used to have some, once.' He tottered away, in search.

'I don't think Tarkus is a Marta, you know,' said Jeremy, in a warning tone.

'No matter, my boy. A little honest fare, to exercise the palate. A good solid platter to keep the wolf at bay. That's all I shall expect at Tarkus's hands.'

Tarkus reappeared. 'This way,' he announced.

They followed him through to a dismal, damp-walled, rotten-beamed, foul-smelling kitchen. There on a table was their meal.

There was a pitcher of water; a huge chunk of old, hard and mildewed bread: a dish of dry and wrinkled roots; and a tiny, little bowl of wretched forest fruit.

Chegwith Skillett coughed. Then he looked most depressed. Then 'The Machine,' he said, loudly. 'Do you know where it is?'

'I do,' said Tarkus. 'I'lll tell you while you eat.'

'I was afraid of that,' muttered Chegwith Skillett.

But he and Jeremy sat down, and while they choked, spluttered and made faces, slowly, mournfully, Tarkus told them about the Machine. They could find it at the end of the path, he said.

'So why haven't you gone yourself?' said Skillett. 'To make yourself happy, once and for all?'

Firstly, said Tarkus, the way wasn't safe. It passed right through the City. The City meant the Hordes.

'A city,' spat Chegwith Skillett, *'here*?'

Yes, said Tarkus, there was, and a splendid city it once had been. It had been full of grand buildings. The people had been grand. They'd had grand ideas and dreams. They'd done grand things.

'Just the place for me,' said Skillett, 'in fact.'

But that was in the past, said Tarkus. The plans went wrong. The buildings fell down. The City came apart. Its people turned into the Hordes.

'What do you mean?'

The people had changed. They grew dirty. Crazy. Savage. Weird. Wicked. Vile. They'd dug tunnels everywhere, for instance, and lived in them, as often as not. Then they started attacking everyone. They'd done it to Tarkus. To Skillett himself.

'I should think,' added Tarkus, 'that that is how he died.'

'Killed by the Hordes?'

'I suppose so, yes.' But Tarkus would still have taken the path, if . . .

'If what?'

'If I'd had the key.'

'Key?' said Jeremy, catching Skillett's eye.

'You need a special key to start the Machine. That's what Skillett always said.' Tarkus looked at them, closely. 'There were just two copies of the key. One was always in his pocket. The other he'd hidden, I don't know where.'

Jeremy looked at his friend again. Chegwith Skillett winked. 'So the keys,' said Skillett, loudly, 'would seem to be lost.' Tarkus agreed. 'And no one can ever use the Machine.' Unless, said Tarkus, a key were found. 'So you can't be put out of your misery.' Tarkus shook his head, and looked very doleful.

'Nonetheless,' said Skillett, with a wily look in his eyes, 'I should be *very interested* to get a glimpse of this Machine. I think it would be *very interesting*. *Interesting enough*, in fact, for us to think of braving the Hordes. Don't you agree?' and he kicked Jeremy – who had been nodding anyway – under the table, very vigorously.

'Ow . . . oh . . . yes!' said Jeremy, glaring at Chegwith Skillett, fiercely.

'So that,' said Skillett, 'is what we will do, Tarkus, old fellow. We will go and have a peek at this Happiness Machine. Now, I think we've had enough of your . . . um . . . generous repast.' Jeremy nodded, eagerly.

'Enough?' said Tarkus.

'Quite enough.'

'You don't want more?'

'Enough,' said Skillett, grimly, 'is as good as a feast.'

'I *always* want more of *something*. Though it's never food, of course.'

'Of course,' said Chegwith Skillett, with a bitter laugh. 'Now, have you got somewhere where we can sleep?'

Tarkus had. Slowly, creakily, groaning as he went, he led them up the gloomily creaking and groaning stairs, and then down a long, long, mouldridden corridor. They reached a room with an unhinged door. Tarkus ushered them in. There were two little beds with no bedclothes; a cracked bowl and jug with no water in; a great, dark cupboard with a yawning door; and a mirror that was all brown blotch. Jeremy glanced through the dirty, little window. Outside, there was nothing but pitch black night.

Tarkus said goodbye, and left. As soon as he was gone, Jeremy rummaged through his pack, and found the key. He held it up in the air, in triumph.

'I bet that's what it's for!' he said, excitedly. 'Your father left it for *you* to find! He wanted *you* to use the Machine!'

Chegwith Skillett got very excited, too. 'So it would seem,' he said. He started hurrying from wall to wall. 'A Machine,' he cried, 'just for me!' Then he tripped on a floorboard, and fell. 'The trouble is,' he said, from the floor, 'that if the Machine was for me, my father lied to everyone else.' He scrambled up again. 'I can't believe that he did, you know. My father – like myself – was a man of honour. He would have done nothing to demean the clan.'

'What clan?'

'The Skillett clan.'

'Since when was there a clan?'

'Since I made it up, just a moment ago. The Honour of the Skilletts. I must maintain it, you know.'

103

'You can't just make up a clan, like that.' Jeremy lay down on his bed, pulled up his knees and snuggled into his jacket. 'But I suppose we'll find out the truth tomorrow. If we can slip past the Hordes.'

Chegwith Skillett collapsed on his bed. 'The Hordes,' he said, 'will be no match for Skillett . . . of the Skilletts. For the Napoleon of . . . Balloonists.'

'Are you *still* the Napoleon of Balloonists? Even without your balloon?'

'I . . . am.'

'Well, you've got to be something different, tomorrow. The Marco Polo of the Path. The Caesar of the City.'

'You,' yawned Skillett, 'are a . . . brainy . . . brat.'

'That's what we'll need, if we're going to get through.' There was silence. 'Chegwith?' said Jeremy. 'Are you listening?'

But Chegwith Skillett was fast asleep. In a few moments, he began to snore. Very loudly.

'But what are you *really*?' said Jeremy, after a while. He concentrated, very hard. 'You're just the . . . Hercules of . . . Hornblowers.' He was pleased with himself, and chuckled. And then he went straight to sleep.

Chapter Eight

But he didn't sleep well. The wind howled, softly.
The house seemed to grate, creak and moan, all on
its own, like a huge creature in pain. Jeremy tossed
and turned. His dreams – or rather, nightmares –
came in fits and starts. He dreamt that something
was in their room, some fearsome shape that
padded around on errands of its own, and then
came looming up towards him. In his dream, he
found he couldn't move. The fearsome shape
peered down. Jeremy struggled. He couldn't get
up, or even turn. Then he dreamt that he woke,
and it was all quite horribly true.

He *was* awake. It was real, all right.

Tarkus was peering down at him. And he had
tied Jeremy to the bed. Jeremy couldn't budge.

'Are you mad?' muttered Jeremy. By way of an
answer, Tarkus brandished the key.

'I *guessed* you would have it,' he hissed, grinning
madly.

'Chegwith!' yelled Jeremy. 'Save me! Help!'

'Huuuuuh. Hum. Worraworra worr?'

'I'm a prisoner, Chegwith! I've been tied to my

bed! Help!'

There was the noise of a big frustrated heave. Then, 'I'm afraid I can't,' said Skillett.

'What's up?'

'I've been tied to my bed, too. Skillett of the Skilletts has been betrayed. By his host, of all people, he must assume. His *host*: the very fellow who should guard his door.'

'Yes,' said Tarkus, modestly, 'it was me.'

'Explain yourself, hell-hound,' said Skillett.

'I came up and searched for the key while you were asleep,' said Tarkus. 'You should have told me you had it, you know.' He sounded hurt.

'What would you have done if we had?'

'I should have stolen it anyway.'

'What do you intend to do now?'

'To get to the Machine, at once. To make myself happy, at last,' and Tarkus clasped the key to his breast, and smiled joyfully at the ceiling.

'And what's going to happen to us?'

'I'll be back before you die,' said Tarkus. 'At least, I might,' and he frowned.

'But what about food and drink?' said Chegwith Skillett. Then 'Forget I said that,' he added, at once.

'I'll be back,' repeated Tarkus. 'And when I come back,' he went on, 'I shall be a changed man. I'll be charming. Good-humoured. I'll be generous and kind. I'll be cheerful and fun. I'll be able to tell you amusing stories. I have never,' said Tarkus, 'told an amusing story in my life before. I shall be the life and soul of the party.'

'The *party*? What party?'

'The big one I'm going to have here.'

'Who's going to come?'

'I shall throw it for myself.'

'Of course you'll be the life and soul,' said Skillett. 'You'll be the only one there.'

'You wait and see,' said Tarkus, and he went.

'But I don't want to!' bawled Chegwith Skillett. 'I don't *want* to come to your party, thanks very much all the same!'

'Supposing you get caught by the Hordes!' yelled Jeremy. 'Supposing they kill you! What's going to happen to us then?'

There was silence.

'In that case,' said Chegwith Skillett, 'in days to come, they will find two skeletons tied to two beds. And they will look at the larger one in awe, and say: "What a splendid specimen was here undone."'

'They might feel sorrier for the little one,' Jeremy objected.

'I doubt it,' Skillett went on. 'For the larger one will be the remains of a Skillett of the Skilletts. It will be a Skilletton.'

There was a long pause. Then 'What an awful pun,' said Jeremy.

'I thought it was rather good myself,' said Chegwith Skillett. 'In the circumstances, at any rate. And talking about the circumstances . . .'

'Yes?'

'I'm going back to sleep,' and he did.

So Jeremy went back to sleep, too. But at dawn they were awake again: a clear, chill dawn.

'Are you thinking what I'm thinking?' said Chegwith Skillett.

'I doubt it,' said Jeremy. 'What a horrible idea.'

'If I were disposed to rise,' said Chegwith Skillett, ' – or rather, if I were able to – I should hammer you.'

'What were you thinking?'

'I was thinking this: our chances of survival seem somewhat slim.'

'Yes.'

'I cannot believe that Tarkus will get there and back.'

'No.'

'Especially not with these menacing Hordes about.'

'Exactly.'

'In which case . . .'

'Yes?'

'It is time to set our minds on higher things.'

'What are you on about?'

Chegwith Skillett fastened his eyes devoutly on

the ceiling. Then he winked, and pointed to the window.

There was a chugging noise coming from the sky. It was distant, right now, but it was getting closer, too.

'It's them!' exclaimed Jeremy. 'Aeronauts Anonymous! They've got the planes going, again!'

'Well, some of the planes, anyway,' said Skillett. 'That doesn't sound like them all.'

The noise got rapidly louder. After a while, it was right above the hall. The planes circled twice, then landed. The engines went quiet.

'Three cheers for our Aeronaut pals,' breathed Chegwith Skillett. 'Assuming – that is – that it's no one else.'

They listened as the front door creaked.

'Well,' said Skillett, 'do we let them know we're here?'

'We haven't any choice,' said Jeremy, and he started bellowing like mad. Chegwith Skillett joined in. The noise echoed away down the corridor.

They kept on shouting. To start with, no one came. But then they heard footsteps hurrying along.

It was Theresa and The Chunterer.

'I knew it!' crowed Theresa, as she helped The Chunterer to untie them both.

'You couldn't have,' said Jeremy.

'I meant that I knew it was us who would find you. Lankin mended our planes first. So we wanted to set off right away. But Bette forbade us, of course.'

'So you disobeyed her, again.'

'Sort of,' said Theresa, giggling. 'When Bette gives orders, you see, it's always in that special voice.'

'What voice?'

'The hateful one,' said Theresa. 'The one that makes you want to say no.'

'Hn,' said The Chunterer, 'hn thn.'

'The Chunterer agrees,' said Theresa.

'But he always agrees with you,' said Jeremy. The Chunterer smiled sweetly at Theresa.

'Hum,' said Theresa. 'But it was him who thought of it. Thought to come down to the house. Whenever there's a problem . . .'

'He turns up trumps.'

'Exactly,' said Theresa. 'Now tell us what happened.'

'I knew it,' said Theresa, when Jeremy had finished.

'You *couldn't* have,' Jeremy exclaimed.

'You,' said Theresa, 'are a tiresome brat. I meant that I knew I was going to disobey again.'

'How d'you mean?'

'Bette said to wait if we found you. But I think we ought to go on. We need to stop Tarkus before he gets to the Machine.'

'We do indeed,' said Chegwith Skillett.

'But how do we follow him, that's the thing.'

'We just keep track of the path. It'll take us all the way to the Machine. But we'll have to go through the City.'

'Why?'

'Because the path goes through it, Tarkus said. Tarkus may be there, and Tarkus has the key.'

Theresa shivered. 'I would rather steer clear of this City,' she said.

'Do not fear,' said Chegwith Skillett, and he folded his arms, and looked very solemn. 'Be they ever so legion, the Hordes will be no match for Skillett the Great. Skillett the Proud! Skillett the Magnificent!!'

'Skillett the Nutter,' said Theresa. 'Let's go.'

So they hurried away to the planes, and took off. It was morning, but the sky was dreary and dark. There were great black clouds humped everywhere. As they went on, it got darker, too, until it felt almost like night again. Below, the forest got thicker and thicker. They could barely make out the path.

Before very long, they caught sight of the City – and gaped.

The City must have been splendid, once. There were spires and domes and columns and arches;

lots of great halls, and palaces, too. The dark, stone buildings were solid and grand. But then they saw the ruined walls. They saw the gaps where the roofs should have been. They saw all the towers that had collapsed. Lots of the buildings were empty shells. Many were just piles of debris on the ground.

Theresa gave a shout, and pointed.

There was a long, wide street beneath them. It wasn't clogged with rubble, like most of the other streets. That – of course – would be the place to land.

So Theresa and The Chunterer took the planes down. As soon as they'd come to a halt, Chegwith Skillett leapt out, and glared boldly around the street, from side to side and then from end to end. But the place seemed utterly deserted. Here a door yawed. There a window gaped. Grass and weeds – even saplings – were springing from every corner and crack. You could look through holes in the blackened walls to other walls and other holes. But there seemed to be no one about.

'*Hordes?*' said Skillett. He flourished the walking-stick, and paced up and down. 'Where are they, then? *Emerge*,' he hollered, '*and confront me, Hordes!*'

'I expect they will,' said Theresa, tartly. 'They wouldn't want to miss you, after all.'

'Why is everything so black?' whispered Jeremy.

'It's soot,' said Theresa. 'There must have been

terrible, terrible fires.'

'But Tarkus didn't say they'd been attacked.'

'Perhaps they started the fires themselves.' Theresa looked up at the dismal, leaden sky, and trembled a little.

'I thought you were an air ace,' said Jeremy.

'I am,' said Theresa.

'Daredevil-in-chief. That's what Bette said.'

'That's correct. That's what I am.'

'I don't think daredevils shake like that.'

'I'm a very brave daredevil,' said Theresa, stiffly, 'so long as I'm in the air. It's coming down to earth that can make me afraid. It's seeing what you see down here.'

'Well,' said Skillett, 'it has to be seen,' and he strode across the street, very fast, whirling his stick in one hand.

Which direction should they go in?

'To the centre,' said Theresa, 'I think.' She looked around, and trembled again.

'What centre?' Jeremy asked.

'I saw it as we flew in,' Theresa explained. 'A great round ring sort of place. It's over that way, if I remember rightly,' and she pointed.

So the four of them set out. They passed through one empty, blackened, silent street, and another. Then the figures began to appear.

They flickered here and there through the empty buildings: filthy, wild-haired women and men.

They dashed from house to house, and clambered over piles of stone. There were lots of them, but they made not a sound. It was like being tracked by a crowd of flitting ghosts.

And then they vanished.

The flyers rubbed their eyes.

'Maybe it was just the light,' said Theresa. 'This place is full of shadows. Strange ones, too,' and she trembled, again. 'I'm frightened,' she confessed, at last.

'Me too,' said Jeremy.

'I meant *really and truly* frightened.'

'So did I. How about Skillett of the Skilletts?'

Jeremy shouted, trying to sound as strong as he could. But Chegwith Skillett was strangely quiet. He stared at the bleak, unfriendly walls. He stared at the lowering sky. He heaved a sigh, and plodded on. The others plodded in his wake.

In a very few minutes, the figures were back. They flashed past windows and peered round doors. They scuttled from street to street. They stood on walls, then leapt out of sight. They never came so close that you could see a face. But they were everywhere – for a while. Then they vanished once more.

The flyers turned a corner, and there, in their path, was a weird, little dwarf. He was dressed in a long, ragged coat, a great, tall hat that was almost as big as himself, and he was very dirty indeed. He had long, matted hair, and his skin was covered in blotches and weals. He looked at the friends, and cackled, crazily.

Then he started gibbering, very fast, and pointing all over the place. At times he seemed to threaten. At times he seemed to plead. But most of the time he hardly seemed to see them at all. Then he turned and shuffled off, very fast. He beckoned to them to follow him.

He led them straight to the centre itself.

The outer rim – where they were standing – was a great ring of tall, ruined buildings. Torches flickered from brackets and poles. From the rim,

there were steps to the middle. A dried-up
fountain stood in the circle there.

'What's that?' whispered Jeremy.

'What?' said Theresa. 'It's too dark to see.'

Jeremy pointed to the inner ring.

Right at the centre stood a stake. Someone was
tied to it, too.

All of a sudden, Chegwith Skillett went leaping
down the steps. The others followed him.

It was Tarkus at the stake: Tarkus, bound fast.

He was alive, but there was a terrified look in his eyes. He managed a stifled, choking sound.

The key had been stuffed in his mouth.

The next moment, the air was full of screeches and yells. Mad-eyed people came jumping and tumbling and racing wildly out of the buildings. They streamed into the ring, grabbed the flyers and pinioned them. A few came running with more stakes.

Jeremy's arms were twisted and held. The others were prisoners, too.

'Chunterer,' muttered Jeremy, 'it's time to turn up trumps.' But The Chunterer couldn't even move.

'Bette!' yelled Theresa, in terror, staring upwards. 'Where are you, Bette? I promise I'll never disobey you again!' But nothing appeared in the sky.

'Chegwith!' shouted Jeremy. 'Do something!'

For a moment, Chegwith Skillett looked angry. He even broke free. But then he waved the walking-stick hopelessly in the air.

What, after all, could he do?

Chapter Nine

BIP!

Chegwith Skillett stared in surprise. One of the men around him fell flat. The others drew back.

BIP! BIP! BIP!

Three more men fell.

'This is a piece of good fortune,' Chegwith Skillett observed. 'Someone is bipping the Hordes. He deserves our gratitude. Well done, Bipper!' he roared.

'Chegwith,' shouted Jeremy, 'it's you!'

BIP! BIP! BIP! BIP! Four more of the Hordes went down.

'I can see the point to bipping,' said Chegwith Skillett, 'especially now. But I myself have never bipped in my life.'

'You're pressing the trigger on the walking-stick! It *is* a gun, the way I thought it was!'

Chegwith Skillett looked thoughtful. Then he looked down. The Hordes waited. Chegwith Skillett looked up, and grinned.

BIP! BIP! BIP! BIP! BIP! BIP! BIP! BIP! BIP! BIP! BIP! BIP! BIP! BIP! BIP! BIP! BIP! BIP! BIP! BIP! BIP! BIP! BIP! BIP! BIP! BIP! BIP! BIP! BIP!

BIP! BIP! BIP! BUP!

'*Bup*?' said Chegwith Skillett.

BUP! said the gun.

'Well,' said Chegwith Skillett, 'nothing is perfect.
Though this was the perfect massacre,' and he
waved cheerfully at all the bodies. 'Or so it would
seem.' He pointed the gun at Jeremy.

'Chegwith!' screamed Jeremy. 'No!'

Chegwith Skillett pulled the trigger, and fired.

Nothing happened.

'Just as I thought,' said Skillett. 'It is a gun that is
only meant for the Hordes.'

'Huh,' said Jeremy, still quaking. 'And what if it *hadn't* been, after all?'

'You would have survived,' said Skillett, and he pointed. The first of his victims was starting to stir.

'Which means . . .'

'It's only a stun gun.'

'Which means . . .'

'We'd better run. *Now!*' The Hordes had hung back, but were closing in again.

Jeremy ran to Tarkus, and snatched the key from his mouth. Then he and The Chunterer untied him. Theresa had already started to run. Chegwith Skillett flourished the stick, and went bipping here, there and everywhere.

Slowly – with Chegwith Skillett still using the stick – they edged themselves out of the ring. They edged their way back along the streets which they'd come through. The Hordes kept up with them, stalking noiselessly from wall to wall.

Finally, they reached the planes. Skillett stood guard while the flyers started up. Then he turned to climb in with Theresa. The Chunterer and Tarkus had already gone.

'Watch out!' Jeremy cried.

Hundreds and hundreds of wild, flailing shapes came hurtling towards them.

'I'm taking off *now!*' screamed Theresa.

'But I'm not in yet!' yelled Skillett.

'Too bad!' screeched Theresa. 'Hold on!' And

sure enough, she took off, just like that, with Chegwith Skillett asprawl on one wing, and the Hordes coming lunging from every side.

When they were safely away from the City, Theresa took them down again. Then she, Jeremy and The Chunterer all got out and clustered around her plane. Chegwith Skillett was still gripping the wing. He had a sort of . . . amazed look in his eyes. But he had kept the stick in his hand.

There was a long silence. Everyone waited for Chegwith Skillett to speak.

'I have decided,' said Chegwith Skillett, after a while, still holding on, 'that I shall no longer be the Napoleon of Balloonists. The Napoleon of Balloonists has henceforth retired.'

'What about all those other silly things you thought you were, too?' said Theresa, loosening one of his arms. The Chunterer loosened the other arm, and they lifted Skillett down. Skillett flopped.

'I shall no longer be Skillett of the Skilletts, either,' said Chegwith Skillett, from the ground. 'Nor shall I be the hero of the battlefield, man among men.' The others all nodded approvingly. 'I shall be plain Chegwith Skillett. A bit of a Bipper, perhaps,' and he gazed fondly at the walking-stick, 'but otherwise merely an Ordinary Bloke.'

'Chegwith,' said Jeremy, 'I don't think you could ever be *that*.'

'Well,' said Chegwith Skillett, 'I shall try. I shall do all the things that Ordinary Blokes do. I shall eat potatoes. I shall own a dog. I shall carry a handkerchief, to blow my nose. I shall dig in my garden, every weekend. I shall look at the sky and hum to myself. I shall even hope that I might make friends. I shall engage – for example – in polite conversation. *If* others,' he muttered, 'are polite to me. That boy is a discourteous brat.' Jeremy had yawned, and wandered off. The Chunterer trailed behind him, solemnly.

'Well,' said Theresa. 'I'm changing, too. No more going off on my own. From now on, I shall stay united. *United*. Even with Bette.'

Jeremy stopped in front of Tarkus, and stared. 'Which is the way to the Machine?' he said. Tarkus pointed, silently. 'How much further have we got to go?'

'Not very far,' mumbled Tarkus.

'Cheer up,' said Jeremy. 'After all, we did save you from the Hordes.'

'I shall never tell amusing stories, now,' said Tarkus, sadly.

Chegwith Skillett came stalking up. 'Tarkus,' he said, 'I don't think you would be able to tell a funny story, whatever happened. But do not despair. You may use the Machine, once we've done so ourselves.'

They got into the planes, and took off again.

Before very long they saw a mountain. It was a huge, peaked, whitish-grey mountain. Tarkus pointed towards it. Then he guided them down.

They landed near a pair of high, silver gates. A tall, silver fence stretched away on both sides. In front of the fence, there were big, dark rocks, and miles of strange-looking mounds of earth. Behind it was a strange, bare, cold-looking garden. The garden went on for a very long time, before the slopes of the mountain began.

'According to Skillett,' said Tarkus, 'the Machine is inside the mountain itself.'

'There's something moving in there,' said Theresa, in a warning tone. They went up to the gate, and stared.

Something *was* moving: several things, in fact. A squat, little tank was chugging soundlessly along an endless furrow of earth. A gawky machine was stalking on two thin legs, digging little holes and planting imaginary seeds. A watering-can on wheels was dipping and bowing and pouring out nothing in places where nothing was growing at all. Further off, there was a man.

'Is it your father?' breathed Jeremy. Chegwith Skillett shook his head.

'Then it must be the gardener,' said Jeremy. 'Your father had a *gardener. Here.*'

Chegwith Skillett bellowed loudly at the man. There was no reply.

He was a very odd-looking man. He bent to the ground, picked and scraped, straightened, then bent, jerkily, steadily, over and over again. When his head came up, it always twisted, sharply, once.

They all peered at him, for a very long time. Then they all looked at each other.

The gardener was a machine, too.

'If Skillett is dead,' said Theresa, 'then these machines must just go on and on, day after day, night after night, without anyone to turn them off.' She sighed.

'Well,' said Jeremy, 'we'll do it ourselves.' But

Chegwith Skillett looked anxious.

'Those gates,' he said. 'There's something about them . . . that disturbs me, you know.'

'What do you mean?' said Jeremy.

'Possibly something I recall from my father. Possibly something he said. Maybe merely something I dreamt. But there is something wrong about those gates.'

'Chegwith,' said Jeremy, 'you're mad. Just watch,' and he started off towards the gates.

'Me first,' said a voice. They turned round.

It was Tarkus. He had taken a little gun from The Chunterer's plane, and he was pointing it at them.

'I'm sorry,' said Tarkus.

'I don't believe it,' said Chegwith Skillett. 'Now give me that gun.'

'Oh dear,' said Tarkus. 'I'm afraid I can't.'

'It will be the worse for you.'

'No it won't,' said Tarkus, scratching his great large head. 'It will be the better for me, you see, because I am very, very unhappy, and the Machine will change all that.' He flourished the gun. 'So I have to have the key. Give it to me, please.'

There was silence. No one moved.

'Tarkus,' said Chegwith Skillett, 'I don't think you know how to shoot.'

Tarkus stared at his gun. He peered down the barrel. He rubbed the butt. His hands were shaking, Jeremy could see. Chegwith Skillett inched forwards.

BLAM!

Skillett's helmet flew from his head, and went spinning through the air.

'I *think*,' said Tarkus, slowly, 'that you pull on this little thing, here.'

BLAM! BLAM! BLAM!

Everyone dived for cover. 'All right!' yelled Chegwith Skillett. 'We surrender! Don't get upset!'

'I'm not,' said Tarkus, 'but I want the key.' Reluctantly, Jeremy gave it to him. Tarkus backed towards the gates. At the gates themselves, he paused. 'Don't try to follow,' he shouted, 'or I'll shoot! I will, you know, now I've found out how!'

'I wouldn't go through those gates if I were you!' shouted Skillett. 'I don't know why, but there's something . . .'

'You won't stop me that way!' bawled Tarkus, and he turned and went in. Nothing happened.

Jeremy glared at Chegwith Skillett.

A great gravel path led away into the garden from the gates. Tarkus started off along it. They watched his big, ugly body as it tottered eagerly away.

Suddenly, a huge, monstrous robot appeared from nowhere. It whirred and clicked towards Tarkus, squeaking and screeching as it went. It had great, thick, metal arms and legs and a huge, thick, heavy, metal head. It had shiny, bright, metallic eyes. In the middle of its chest was a cube-shaped hole.

Tarkus stopped in his tracks. He was shaking with fright, and dropped the key.

'*You*,' said the robot, in a grating voice, '*are a miserable intruder.*'

'Y-y-yes,' stammered Tarkus. 'I *am*. I am a very m-m-m-miserable intruder. That's w-w-why I . . .'

'*The path*,' said the robot, '*must be cleansed of you.*' It pointed a finger at Tarkus's head.

'I j-j-j-just wanted to be h-h-h-h-happy,' stammered Tarkus. In his fear, he half fell to the ground.

The robot gave out a fierce chugging sound. Then it clanked, loudly, several times. Tarkus turned, pathetically, and stumbled away, dropping the key. The robot caught him. It pressed his head with its finger, once.

Tarkus just dissolved. Like that. He turned into a floating cloud of specks of grey dust. It descended, slowly, and formed a little pile.

The robot chuffed and clanked again, in a sort of self-satisfied way. Then it crossed its arms on its chest, and went quite still, in the middle of the path.

Jeremy and the others stared. After a while, 'Poor Tarkus,' said Jeremy.

'A wretched creature from beginning to end,' said Chegwith Skillett. 'He was selfish and deceitful . . .'

'But he didn't deserve to *die*,' said Jeremy, tearfully.

Chegwith Skillett swallowed, hard. Then, 'Agreed,' he said. 'I know what you're thinking,' he went on. '*My father* made that horrible Machine.' Jeremy nodded. 'I used to think that my father was a wonderful man. I used to think,' said Chegwith Skillett, 'that my father could do no wrong. But what happened to Tarkus could have happened to me, or you. *My father* . . . what *are* you doing, boy?' he snapped. Jeremy had suddenly run off. He had grabbed the bag containing Skillett's father's junk, and come back. Now he was standing right in front of Chegwith Skillett, and grinning. 'If I were not so distracted,' said Skillett, 'I should wallop you.' Jeremy reached into the bag, and pulled out the cube-shaped plunger.

'Don't you see?' he said.

'Yes,' said Chegwith Skillett, 'I see. I see one of those objects that my father left behind, and that serve no useful purpose at all.'

Jeremy pointed to the robot's chest. 'The hole,' he said, breathlessly. Chegwith Skillett stared, first at the plunger, then at the robot. 'It must be some sort of *key*,' Jeremy went on. 'Something that switches the robot off.'

Chegwith Skillett stared again.

'But it's not just the plunger!' shouted Jeremy,

excitedly. 'The plunger, the key, the walking-stick
. . . Don't you *see*?'

'Yes,' said Chegwith Skillett, 'I see. I see a young
and troublesome boy, too often the bane of my life,
getting far too excited for his own little good.'

'Your father left you all the right things. The
things that would make sure that you and no one
else could get to the Machine. I bet this will come in
handy, as well,' and Jeremy took out the little
flame-thrower. 'And this, too,' and he waved the
tiny barrel-organ in the air. 'You're starting to
doubt your father. But he wanted you to be safe.'

'He didn't much care about Tarkus. Or anyone
else who happened along. Including *you* (as it
might have been),' and Chegwith Skillett took
Jeremy by the hand, and they gazed together at the
little pile of dust. Then Skillett took the plunger
from Jeremy's hand.

'*Halt*!' cried a voice. Skillett halted, and looked.
It was M'Graw.

He emerged from behind a mound, near the
gates. Otto and Errol were at his side. They were
pointing their blunderbusses, and sniggering.
Theresa hid the plunger behind her back.

'So,' said M'Graw, 'my excellent Tracer has
found you again. You must have been most . . .
preoccupied. You seem to have failed to notice our
arrival at all.'

A bunch of little black dots, like flies, appeared in

129

the distant sky. It was the Hookey Bandits. Before very long, they had landed, too. They came scuttling over from their planes.

'Issa *goodies*!' yelled their leader. 'Goodies got cort! Hee . . . ray!'

'Hee . . . ray!' roared the others. 'Rah rah rah! Hee . . . ray! Hee . . . rah! Hee . . . rah rah rah!' They all went running around the captives, poking them here, pulling at them there, and making them feel very uncomfortable indeed.

M'Graw went up to Chegwith Skillett. Otto and Errol went, too.

'You,' said M'Graw, 'were extremely unkind – not to say brutal – to my two best friends.' Chegwith Skillett was silent. Otto and Errol frowned. 'I am tempted to let them loose on you,' said M'Graw. Otto and Errol fingered their weapons, and grinned. 'But I shan't – for the moment, at least.' Otto and Errol looked very disappointed. 'Your father's Machine must be there,' said M'Graw, and he pointed behind the fence. 'It will clearly not be easy to reach,' he added, looking at the robot. 'But if anyone knows how to reach it, it is *you*. So you'd better tell me. Now.'

Chegwith Skillett ground his teeth, clenched his jaws and shook his head.

'I'd advise you to think again,' drawled M'Graw. 'Otto and Errol can be most unpleasant. Especially when provoked.'

Otto and Errol each grabbed one of Chegwith Skillett's wrists. The Hookey Bandits crowded round him, too.

Suddenly, a small clod of earth struck M'Graw on the neck. At the top of one of the strange-looking mounds, there was a tiny uprush of earth.

All at once, a mound erupted. Earth and mud went spraying into the air. Then other mounds erupted, too. Hundreds and hundreds of figures leapt screeching to the ground or came running through the rocks.

Theresa screamed. The Hordes were back on the attack.

They dashed at the group in front of the gates. Chegwith Skillett grabbed his friends and hid them behind a rock. The others were not so fast.

For a moment, M'Graw just stared. Then he howled, and ran for the balloon. Otto and Errol panicked, and fired off their blunderbusses in all directions. Then they ran, too. But the Hookey Bandits decided to stand and fight.

There was a great, stormy hurly-burly in front of the gates: growlings, tearings, snappings, swearings, scratchings, pummellings, threats and pleas. The Hookey Bandits were furious and fierce . . . but few. In the end, they were bound to lose.

After a while, the Hordes drew back. They looked at the bodies on the ground. Then they strutted silently in front of the fence, with vacant, mad, triumphant eyes.

Chegwith Skillett came out from behind his rock. He had the stick in his hand. He waved it in the air, for all to see.

The Hordes assembled. Chegwith Skillett pointed the stick.

The Hordes eyed him, for a very long time. Then, slowly, they started to disperse. Some disappeared into the mounds again. Others sloped away between the rocks. Before very long, the place was empty once more.

Chapter Ten

Jeremy listened. So did his friends. Everything was completely quiet.

'So the Hordes have returned . . . where they came from,' said Chegwith Skillett, bewilderedly.

'The tunnels,' said Jeremy.

'Ah,' said Chegwith Skillett. 'The tunnels. Yes.' He sounded just as puzzled as before.

'Tarkus said they dug tunnels, remember? Well, the mounds must be where the tunnels end.'

'But why do the tunnels all end at the fence?' Jeremy gazed. It was true. There weren't any mounds on the opposite side.

'I can guess,' he said.

'Let us hear.'

'The Hordes knew about the Machine, as well,' said Jeremy. 'They thought it was for them. Everyone seems to do that, you know. So they tried to get to it, but somehow your father kept them out. I think he made some terrible weapon, and it stopped them tunnelling under the fence.'

There was a pause. Then, 'That sounds like a very sensible guess,' Chegwith Skillett remarked.

'To an Ordinary Bloke like myself . . .'

'Oh, shut *up!*' said Jeremy. Suddenly, for some reason, he felt he had had enough; enough of his adventures; enough of the Machine; enough of its inventor; and – above all – enough of his son. He went storming off, and sat down under a rock. Chegwith Skillett looked very surprised. Then he shambled over, meekly. After a while 'Ahem,' he said.

Jeremy was silent.

'You,' said Chegwith Skillett, 'are a temperamental brat. Why so aggrieved, if I might ask?'

'You've been so many things,' said Jeremy. 'Son of the Inventor. The Man who did Nothing. The Napoleon of Balloonists. Skillett of the Skilletts. And now you're an Ordinary Bloke. But they've all been *games*, every single one. And you play games with me, as well. You were making fun of me just now.'

Chegwith Skillett considered. 'Don't you think that playing might be wisdom, at times?'

'Not all the time, about everything.'

'I meant it,' said Skillett. 'It really was a sensible guess. My father was clever, was he not?' Jeremy nodded his head. 'My father was damnably clever. The more I discover, the more I see how damnably, damnably clever he was. But now I want to find out the whys. Why in this place? With the robots and the Hordes? You know what I think?' Jeremy shook his head. 'I think that something was *wrong*.'

And, all at once, Jeremy felt very different. Poor, sad, peculiar, friendless Chegwith. He'd never *known* his Dad. He'd never seen him much. His Dad (perhaps) had hardly cared. But the son had loved him, all the same. Jeremy decided that he felt sorry for Chegwith Skillett, after all. He got to his feet. 'Well,' he said, 'there's only one way to find out. And nothing's going to stop us now.' He took hold of Chegwith Skillett's arm, and they started off towards the gate.

'Wait!' shouted Theresa.

Bette and Lankin's planes were above them in the sky. They were towing Belvedere Jones's balloon. Before very long, they'd landed. The others ran over to meet them, and told them all of their news.

'And, Bette,' said Theresa, humbly.

'Yes,' said Bette, in a frigid sort of voice, looking in the opposite direction.

'You wanted us to stay united.'

'Yes,' said Bette. 'You disobeyed, again.'

'*United*, you said, *at all times*.Well, from now on, I've decided that I will. Stay united, that is,' and she marched up to Bette and held out her hand. Bette peered at it, suspiciously.

'Don't worry,' said Jeremy. 'She means it. Be friends.' So Bette and Theresa shook hands.

Belvedere Jones went up to Chegwith Skillett. The others all listened, respectfully. Jones was smiling. 'Chegwith,' he said, 'you have survived unscathed. This, I presume, is the home of the Machine,' and he gestured languidly with his cane. Skillett nodded. 'So: you are almost at the end of your quest.'

'And it's due to you,' said Chegwith Skillett. Belvedere Jones waved a modest glove. 'It was you who got me to leave Humpidore's.'

'Your father would have wanted it,' said Jones. 'Your father – of course – was a very strange man.' Chegwith Skillett nodded, again. 'No one was ever quite sure what he was up to. But I knew he'd have wanted you to follow his trail. And that is exactly what you have done.'

'Only with your help,' said Skillett. 'You saved us from the Vanishing Point . . .'

Belvedere Jones waved, again. 'It is you,' he said, 'who have stuck to your task. We tried to deter you. You persevered. Since you left the Home, I have watched you grow.' Chegwith Skillett folded his arms. 'You have become resourceful.' Chegwith Skillett put one foot forward. 'You have gained in force and confidence.' Chegwith Skillett thrust back his shoulders. 'You have shown yourself brave in adversity.' Chegwith Skillett threw back his head. 'Chegwith – you are a man transformed.'

'Thank you,' said Skillett. 'But at bottom,' he added, 'I am merely an Ordinary Bloke. Harum-scarum at times, I admit. Unpredictable. Wild, you will say. Not the sort of person you would want next door. Not the sort of man you would ask for as a friend. None the less, I am in fact a plain old sort of fellow who's done a plain old sort of job as best he could. And let me say, here, now, before these others . . .'

'You aren't.' Chegwith Skillett glanced round. It was Jeremy who had spoken.

'What?'

'You aren't before the others. They've all wandered off, except me.' Skillett looked round. It was true. The others were walking towards the gate. Jeremy and Skillett ran after them.

'Stop!' shouted Jeremy. 'Not without the plunger! Don't go in!'

He and Chegwith Skillett ran to the planes, grabbed Skillett senior's odds and ends, stuffed them into a bag, and caught up with the others, as quickly as they could. Then they all stopped at the gateway and stared at the robot. The robot was still standing in the middle of the path, with its arms across its chest. Jeremy fingered the plunger.

'I'll go, if you like,' he whispered. He didn't really mean it, he knew.

'No, my boy,' said Chegwith Skillett, firmly, and he took the plunger from Jeremy's hand. 'My father meant it to be me, you know. And so, you see: it is me it must be.' Slowly, steadily, solemnly, he started off along the great gravel path.

He stopped at the pile of Tarkus dust. He bent, found the key, and pocketed it, swiftly, so that no one saw. The robot waited, motionless. Then it gave out a great big click, and a thump. It whirred and buzzed several times, very fast. It flexed its arms and spun them round. Its eyes flashed twice, metallically.

Chegwith Skillett halted, and watched.

'You have intruded into my domain,' burred the robot.

'There must be some mistake,' said Skillett. 'I am an Ordinary Bloke on an Ordinary Hike.'

'You are not,' said the robot.

'I beg your pardon?' said Skillett, politely.

'You are not a Bloke. You are a Trespasser. The path must accordingly be cleansed of you.' The robot came lurching forwards, squeaking and screeching as it came. Skillett fingered the key.

The robot came on. It spread its arms. It loomed and hunched above its prey.

Suddenly, Chegwith Skillett launched himself forwards. He thrust the plunger straight into the robot's chest. The robot hugged him close.

And then, with a clank, one of its arms fell off. The second fell, with another clank. Smoke came spouting from the robot's ears. It spun around once, wailing harshly, like a crazy, wounded animal in horrible pain. Then it went spinning wildly off the path, moulting metal panels as it went. It coughed, several times, and its head went flying off. At last it collapsed in a sprawling, ungainly heap.

Rapidly, quietly, the friends tiptoed by, collecting Chegwith Skillett as they went.

They went on through the bare, chilly garden. They aimed for the mountain, as Tarkus had said. For quite some time, there was little to see. Then they reached a high, stone wall.

There seemed to be no way in.

Belvedere Jones leant a little on his cane. 'Ah Skillett,' he murmured. 'You make things so *hard*.' The others had all sat down, in despair. Skillett the Younger looked at Jeremy.

'The plunger has gone,' he said. 'And in any case – it was hardly likely to open a wall.'

'I don't think the flame-thrower or the little barrel-organ will do that, either,' said Jeremy, looking forlornly at their last two aids.

Chegwith Skillett flew into a rage. 'Dad!' he bellowed. 'You rotten, horrible swine!' He went running to the wall, and shook his fists in the air. 'You aren't playing fair! I don't know what you were doing here! I've no idea what it's all about! But I know you wanted me to find this! I know you wanted me to reach your Machine! Yet you almost killed me with your robot, and now – well, you're just tormenting me! So stop it! Stop it, right away! Just *open up!*'

Nothing happened.

'He's dead, remember,' said Jeremy, softly.

'I know,' said Chegwith Skillett. 'But at times like this I remember his power, and I think that he can't be, *really*,' and he prodded forlornly at the wall with his boot.

There was a sound that was almost like a grating laugh. A little door swung open to Chegwith Skillett's foot.

'You see?' whispered Chegwith Skillett. 'It's as if he were teasing from beyond the grave.'

The door was a *very* little door. Jeremy himself could get through it, he knew. He wasn't so sure about the rest.

But Bette crawled through it all right. Theresa went through, and Lankin and The Chunterer. Belvedere Jones knelt daintily on the ground, and he crawled through, too, clutching his cane as he went. Then Chegwith Skillett bent and kneeled.

He was wearing his great, thick jacket. He forgot to take it off.

Chegwith Skillett got stuck.

So Jeremy found that, once again, he was staring at the loud check trousers. At the bottom with which this had all begun. The bottom wriggled, feverishly. But it stayed stuck.

Jeremy thought for a while. Then, very deliberately, he lifted his foot, and pushed with his heel, very hard, several times.

The bottom went through, with a yowl. Jeremy crawled through after it.

Chegwith Skillett was lying face down on the ground, with his nose in a pool of mud. Jeremy walked round and gazed at the top of Chegwith Skillett's head.

There was silence. Then 'Uth uh wur nuth un thur grund,' said Chegwith Skillett, with his face still in the mud, 'ur ruthur, uth yur wur dun hur, uth shud *murdur* yur.' The others picked him up, and cleaned him down. Then they all looked about them, and gaped.

They were standing in an inner garden – and a strange little garden it was.

It was very neat, and, well . . . *fancy*, muttered Bette. But nothing in it was natural at all. They started to walk. They passed by row upon row of plastic flowers. The petals glittered dully in the sullen light. They gazed up into tinsel-looking trees. Here and there, in the branches, they spotted mechanical birds. The birds did mechanical flutters and bends, and pecked like little power drills, and squawked like unoiled cogs. Chubby plastic statues grinned through metal bushes, and a fountain spouted a jet of white dust. There was even a pond that was made of a kind of glass, with plump, dummy carp that wagged in place. There were more mechanical gardeners, too. A featureless fellow prodded slowly at a rockery. A second dangled a rod and line over a glass-topped stream. A third tied creepers like wires across a trellis of silver tubes.

'Look,' breathed Bette. Fluttering towards them, soaring and sinking through the chilly air, was a cluster of small, bright, metal butterflies. They had beautiful, shimmering wings, and their colours seemed to ebb and change as they went. They reached the friends, and hovered there above their heads. Everyone looked up, entranced.

'How pretty,' said Theresa, dreamily. 'How very pretty,' she murmured, again.

The butterflies started to grow. Their little black heads began to swell. You could see their pinpoint, steely eyes.

'Watch out!' screamed Jeremy. The very next moment, he had to duck. Something banged on his shoulder, hard.

The butterflies were attacking them! They were flapping down viciously, with giant wings. Jeremy struggled back up again. Lankin had been beaten to the ground. The Chunterer was tottering wildly, here and there, screeching, with a butterfly clinging leech-like to his neck. Belvedere Jones was fending off three by jabbing frantically with his cane.

'Chegwith!' yelled Jeremy. Chegwith Skillett was surrounded. 'Try the flame-thrower!' Skillett grabbed something from the bag. Then he fell over backwards. The butterflies closed in.

All of a sudden, there was a loud SSSSSSSSS! A long tongue of fire went leaping into the air.

One of the butterflies curled at the edges, then crumpled in, melted, turned black, and dropped in a lump to the ground. SSSSSSSSS! A second did the same. Chegwith Skillett downed the others around him. He went over to Belvedere Jones, and downed his butterflies, too. Then he tramped about, loosing off the flame-thrower here, there

143

and everywhere until the butterflies were all just scraps of charred and twisted junk. Chegwith Skillett lowered the flame-thrower, and solemnly surveyed the scene.

The others crowded around him, too.

'I said my father was damnably clever, did I not?' said Chegwith Skillett, to Jeremy.

'You did,' said Jeremy.

'I'm beginning to believe he was damnably wicked, too.'

'But he left you the flame-thrower. He wanted you to survive.'

'That,' said Chegwith Skillett, 'is not the point. My father made those devilish creatures. My father made them able to kill,' and he stared in distress at the sombre sky.

'Let us move on,' said Belvedere Jones, in a soothing voice. 'I do not suggest it (dear Chegwith) because of any interest in your father's Machine. But it is there that you may find your explanation, in the end.'

So they went on through the garden, watching out for more butterflies, until the mountain was looming right above them. At last, they arrived at its lower slopes. There in its side was a great, dark door.

'We haven't got a key for *that*, you know,' said Chegwith Skillett, anxiously. But the door just opened to the touch.

They went inside, and on, down a corridor that was very long and very dark. At last, at the end, they saw a little light.

It was a kind of small hallway, with a sparkling, silver door at the end. A row of wooden figures stood on either side. All of them were characters from stories. Jeremy recognized some.

There was Hansel opposite Gretel. Punch faced Judy, and Peter Pan Wendy, the Owl faced the Pussy-Cat and Jack faced the Giant. There was Tweedledum and Tweedledee, the Prince and Cinderella, Harlequin and Columbine and Beauty and the Beast. There were lots of others, too. They all stood there, very stiffly, as though they were waiting for something.

Suddenly, there was a loud rattling noise. A figure on a trapeze came shooting down a track from above the door. It reached the end of the rows of figures, and stopped above Chegwith Skillett's head. It hung there, swaying back and forth.

The figure looked down, jerkily. It was a wooden woman in a tight gold suit. She had red cheeks, a very red mouth, a very white face and stony blue eyes. She giggled, raucously, twice.

'I'm afraid you cannot enter,' she said. 'Entry is forbidden, you see. There is no way through. None at all.' She laughed once more. Her laugh echoed

down the tunnel, and away. 'My friends below me will see to that.'

Chegwith Skillett laughed in his turn. 'What?' he said. 'They're dummies, just like you,' and he stepped forwards a pace, between the two lines.

There was a swooping, rushing, clicking noise. The figures began to move, very fast. They turned and twisted and arched and flexed. Peter Pan's thumb turned into a dirk. A rapier appeared in Columbine's hand. The Pussy-Cat raised a bludgeon, with spikes. The others brandished knives, whips, clubs and spears. They poised their weapons, waiting to strike.

'Do not go any further,' said the woman on the trapeze, and she giggled again.

'Chegwith,' whispered Jeremy, in terror, 'don't move an inch.'

'I-I-I'm afraid . . . I've *got* to, you know,' said Chegwith Skillett. Very, very slowly, he raised the bag to his chest. Columbine's rapier advanced towards him. Very, very slowly, Chegwith Skillett reached inside. The rapier slanted up towards his throat. Skillett brought out the barrel organ. The rapier pressed at his neck.

'Well,' said Chegwith Skillett, in a strangled sort of way, 'here goes.' He grasped the handle, and began to turn.

The barrel-organ started to play its sweet, little, haunting, tinkly tune. For a moment, the rapier trembled. Then it began to withdraw. The weapons all shrank back into their holders. The rows of figures shuffled forwards. Stiffly, they curtseyed and bowed. Stiffly, they all linked hands. Their arms went stiffly round each others' backs. Stiffly, they began to dance.

Chegwith Skillett sighed a huge sigh of relief, and carried on turning. He and the others threaded their way through the dance, and got as far as the shining door. Then – with Skillett still playing to the last – they turned and went in.

Chapter Eleven

THE DREAM MACHINE

That was what they saw.

They were in a great, big, windowless chamber, with a rounded ceiling and curving sides. It was lit by a dim yellow glow that was coming from the floor. The walls were covered in equipment: boxes, small and large, with red and orange lights; levers and switches and meters and wires; and lots and lots of white tubes, running here, there and everywhere. A set of tall, white metal cases was standing in a corner. There was a large dark air-shaft to one side, and screens and diagrams hung from the walls. A steady, low hum was all around them, like the hum of an engine that's waiting to start.

In the middle of it all was the Machine.

The Machine was large, white, as tall as a street light, and shaped like an egg-timer. It bristled with antennae and aerials, and had several portholes, and a door. The door was glass, and they could see

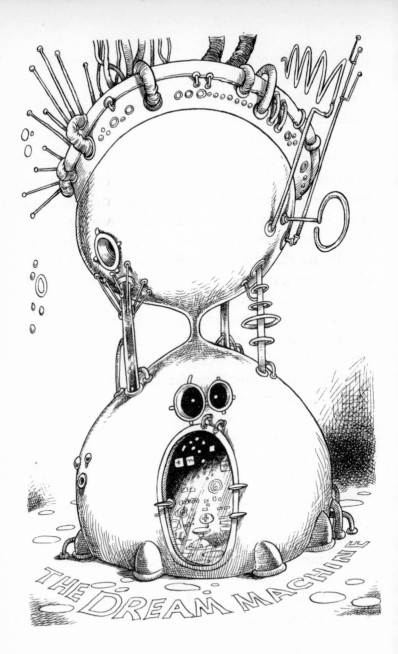

THE DREAM MACHINE

inside to a dimly lit compartment that was full of panels and screens and buttons and knobs. Around the Machine, on the floor, was a glowing circle of orange light. It was flashing up the words: THE DREAM MACHINE.

'So that's what it is,' breathed Jeremy. 'A *dream* machine. And I bet that means,' he added, with excitement, 'that it can make people's dreams come true. That's why everyone thought it was for them.' He clapped his hands. 'Oh, Chegwith, now I really am glad that you took me with you, after all. Just imagine. I can have everything I want . . .'

'No,' boomed a voice, 'I'm afraid you can't.' It was an oddly hollow-sounding voice. They all looked round. M'Graw came strolling from the air-shaft. Otto and Errol were behind him. They were covered in dust, and their blunderbusses were pointing straight at Jeremy and his friends.

'How did *you* get here?' said Chegwith Skillett, in amazement. 'I mean, *we* nearly died, and *you* . . .'

'Very simple,' yawned M'Graw. 'You remember I told you about my Drill?' The others shook their heads. 'The second of my best inventions, you know. I realized the Machine had to be in the Mountain. So all I had to do was to land, and tunnel down. Which I did with great speed. Thanks to the Drill.'

'And where are the Hookey Bandits?' asked Chegwith Skillett.

'The Hookeys?' sniffed M'Graw. 'I thought they were best left behind. Think what they would do in a place like this. Can you imagine their dreams come true?' He shuddered a little, then composed himself. 'An appalling prospect, I'm sure you'll agree.'

'And *your* dreams, M'Graw?' said Skillett, stiffly.

'Ah. *My* dreams. Now *they're* a different affair. Though they're not in fact as wicked as you might suppose. Wealth. Pleasure. Doing what I like. You see,' drawled M'Graw, 'I have grown *so* tired of the inventor's life. So much work, with so little reward. So much *thought*,' and he laughed. 'I think it is time to enjoy myself. If others have to suffer . . . then suffer they shall,' and he walked to the edge of the circle on the floor. 'Otto. Errol. Watch them, now,' and he stepped across the edge of the glowing ring.

All at once, there was a fizzing, crackling sound, and the lights went on and off, very fast. M'Graw was enveloped in a cloud of smoke. There was a scuffling sound. A lot of squat, pot-bellied robots seemed to appear from nowhere. They all had sticks in their hands and they scuttled up to M'Graw and his cronies and started beating them, hard. Otto and Errol yowled, dropped their weapons and ran for the tunnel. M'Graw gave a very loud screech, and started running, too. The robots scurried after them. The yowling and screeching echoed away. Then there was silence.

The others waited for a while. 'I do believe,' said Skillett, 'that Dad has finally put paid to M'Graw.'

'Yes,' said Jeremy, 'I think he has.'

'The question is: will Dad also put paid to me?' Chegwith Skillett gave the Machine a wary, sidelong glance.

'Chegwith,' said Jeremy, anxiously, 'don't try. I mean: I'd love to have my dreams come true. But how's the Machine going to know it's you?'

'I have no idea,' said Chegwith Skillett.

'I've decided I agree with you. Your dad was really mean. Look at all his horrible tricks. Maybe you'll be risking your life. And . . . and . . . well, I'm fond of you, you know,' and Jeremy clung to Chegwith Skillett's arm.

Chegwith Skillett looked down. 'Fond?' he muttered.

'Yes.'

'Really? *Fond?*'

'Of course.'

'Do you mean fond . . . as in *like?*'

'As in really, really like a lot.'

Chegwith Skillett looked down sheepishly at his spindly legs; at his feet in their tattered, old black boots. 'I don't think anyone's been that,' he muttered. '*Fond*. Before this. Of *me*, that is.'

'Well,' said Jeremy, 'we all are. It's just that you haven't noticed, up till now. So . . . don't risk it. *Please.*'

Theresa coughed. 'Maybe someone else should try,' she said. 'Maybe someone . . . like Bette.'

'I thought you were friends,' said Jeremy.

'We are,' said Theresa. 'I want *her* to get all the glory, you see.' But Chegwith Skillett shook his head.

'Then it has to be me,' said Belvedere Jones. Chegwith Skillett shook his head again. 'I really think that it *should*, you know.' Jones's voice was snarling and strange. Jeremy looked up.

Belvedere Jones was leaning on his cane. There was a smile on his lips, and a pistol in his hand.

'Mr Jones,' said Jeremy, stupidly. 'It's *us*.' Jones went on pointing the pistol.

'You,' he said, 'are a stupid little brat.'

'I don't think *he's* very fond of me,' said Chegwith Skillett. Then, all of a sudden, his eyes bulged wide. He threw his head back, and gave a great guffaw. Then he snorted, ferociously. 'Well I never!' he cried. 'I understand, now! You made it all happen, didn't you? Belvedere Jones. You came and got me from Humpy's. You set me off, and then you waited, and watched. Of course, you had to save me from the Vanishing Point. But otherwise you just bided your time, and let me take all the risks.' He made as if to jump. Belvedere Jones waved the pistol, and laughed. Chegwith Skillett choked back his rage. 'Just tell me one thing. How did you know I'd get here in the end?'

Belvedere Jones looked at him, hard. 'Because your father knew,' he said, at last.

'He told you I would?'

'No. But I guessed. Your father, you see, was a brilliant man. Quite, quite brilliant. Beyond compare. I knew he'd be too clever for the rest of us. And I knew it was you – and only you – that he would have wanted to reach the Machine. I knew he would trust you to do it, too, somehow, in some way. And you did.'

'He knew me better than I knew myself.' Chegwith Skillett hung his head.

Belvedere Jones gave a lazy nod. 'He knew a very great deal.'

'So you killed him,' spluttered Chegwith Skillett. 'For *this*,' and he gestured round.

'This?' said Jones, flourishing his cane. '*This?* Do you know what *this* means?' The circle on the floor was dark. Jones backed over it, still pointing the pistol. He backed up against the Machine, then patted it, fondly, watching them. His eyes went crazy and hooded and dark. '*Power!* Power over everything! The whole of the world, if that's what I decide! Your Dad might not have wanted it. But I most certainly do!'

'You killed him,' said Skillett, grimly, 'all the same.'

'No,' said Jones. 'I did not. I might have wished to, but that's another matter. I don't know how he died. But his misfortune . . .'

'Is your good luck?' said Skillett. He patted his pocket, just once. 'I wouldn't touch that door, if I were you.'

'I'm afraid I shall,' said Jones. He took hold of the handle, and pulled.

The door didn't open. Jones tried again; again, no good. Then he tried to let go.

His hand stayed stuck to the door.

Jones pulled, gently at first, then fiercely, then madly, despairingly, frenziedly. He dropped his cane, and tried to prise himself free. Still no good.

He stood stock still, looking dreadfully afraid.

WHAM! Something seemed to pass through him, like a vast electric shock. His clothes disappeared. His hair stood up on end. His jaw dropped, his cheeks swelled and his eyes came popping out of his head. His skin turned transparent. Inside it, every vein and nerve was glowing, like the coils on an electric fire. Then the power died away. The skin sagged, like a punctured balloon, with a squeal. All that was left

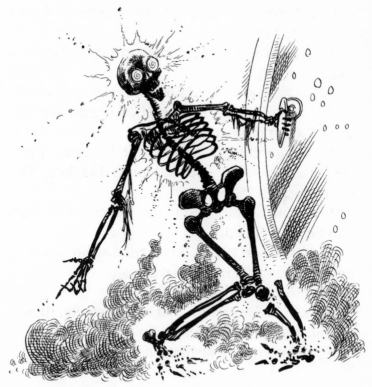

was a black skeleton. It tottered forwards; one pace; two. Then it toppled to the ground, with the clink of falling skittles, and lay there, in bits.

The others goggled. Chegwith Skillett stepped forwards.

'Chegwith,' said Jeremy, 'no.'

'I have the key,' said Skillett.

'I know,' said Jeremy. 'But even so . . . you really can't trust that machine.'

'I'm afraid I must,' said Skillett.

'Chegwith . . .' said Theresa.

'Stop!' said Lankin. 'Ahaw! Stop there!'

'We don't think you should do it!' put in Bette.

'Wn thn,' said The Chunterer. 'Ngn thn thn, wn thn thn yn thn stn rhn thn. Thn thn gn un un thn thrn, wn thn thn yn thn dn.'

The others looked astonished. 'Wasn't that splendid?' said Theresa. 'I don't think we've ever heard him say that much.'

'Not in a month,' added Bette.

'Un thn,' said the Chunterer, fervently. 'Bn un thn thn, Chn Skn mn . . .'

'It's all right, Chunterer,' said Bette. 'We care, too.' Chegwith Skillett held up a hand.

'My friends,' he said. 'I thank you for your concern. Now, I see that you really *are* . . . fond was the word?' he whispered. Jeremy nodded his head. '*Fond*. Of . . . me. But there is nothing else to turn to. M'Graw is gone. Jones is dead. I have met all the others I needed to meet. The Machine alone will tell me more. And there's still some more to find out, you see.' He looked so very firm and determined that no one spoke again. Skillett turned, and walked steadily towards the door. His friends all stood there, fearfully, and watched.

Skillett took the key from his pocket. He found the lock, and inserted the key. Slowly, gently, he turned his hand.

'Go no further.'

A strange figure seemed to form in the air. It drifted across to Skillett, and hovered there in front of him. It was a man; yes, it was a man all right, but his form was ringed in a halo of light. It was the halo you noticed first. Then you noticed the face. It was a wise and wicked and wonderful face, with lines that spread out everywhere, and eyes that were fierce and funny and cunning and kind, all at once.

'Chegwith,' said the man.

'*Dad*,' breathed Chegwith Skillett, and his eyes shone.

'I know it is you. Do not go on. The Machine is booby-trapped. From end to end. Over and over and over again.'

'Oh Dad. I'm so pleased to see you. But why have you laid so many traps?'

Chegwith's father seemed not to hear him. 'I wanted you to find me,' he said. 'You have.'

'Dad? Can you hear me?'

'I expect you had to fend off M'Graw. Others as well, perhaps. Belvedere Jones, I have no doubt.'

'Can you *see* me? Dad?'

'But I'm afraid I have bad news. This isn't me.'

Chegwith Skillett slumped to the floor. 'I thought not,' he moaned.

'This is just a picture. Like a recording or a film. Simply more real, of course.' Chegwith Skillett put his face in his hands. 'I know that this will disappoint you. But I'm afraid you won't see your father again.'

Chegwith Skillett lay down on the floor. 'Listen.

I'll explain just once.' Chegwith Skillett sat up again. 'Then I'll be silent for good. You see before you,' said the figure, smiling, 'the results of a lifetime's work. My life, that is. *The Dream Machine*. Many years ago, I decided to make one. I have thought of nothing else, ever since. That was why – Chegwith – you saw me so seldom. I dreamt and worked and planned and laboured. Day and night, when others were sleeping or having their fun, I worked. A Dream Machine – I said to myself – was just what everyone needed, you see. It would bring all kinds of good to the world. Just imagine it, Chegwith . . . a machine to make everyone's dreams come true! and I succeeded, as well!'

Then the wonderful, wrinkled face looked sad. The voice went quiet. The shoulders drooped. The image faded, a little. It looked more like a ghost than it had before.

'But I had to give up,' it said, and it hung its head. It paused for a moment, then looked up again. 'The trouble was,' it went on, 'that not all dreams are the same. Some people's dreams are little: dreams for themselves, and the people they love. But other people's dreams are big. They stretch to cover *everything*. They are horrible dreams; or have horrible results.' The figure looked most distressed.

'But as far as the Machine went, dreams were dreams. It couldn't tell one kind from the other, you see. I tried to make it, but it wouldn't. No matter how hard I worked. All or nothing, it kept on saying. You can't have some without the rest. So I realized.' The voice went plaintive and small. 'My Machine had become a menace, in fact.' The figure bowed its head once more. It stayed that way, for a very long time.

'So all that work . . . and no one would use it. I felt so *angry* and bitter. I said that I would get my own back on anyone who got this far. I invented all my devilish traps. But I knew you would survive them, and I wanted you to get here. I wanted you to *understand*, you see.'

The figure raised its head, and smiled. 'But by the time you understand, I shall be gone. I have decided to try out the Machine, just once. Try it out with one of *my* dreams. I knew I could trust them, at least. But it's not a dream from which I can return.' The ghost was fading fast.

Chegwith Skillett leapt to his feet. 'Is that really all you've got to say?' he roared. 'After I've come so far? After you've left me on my own like this? You wanted me to understand! What about thinking of *me*?'

'Sorry, Chegwith . . .' The ghost was thinning to a shapeless haze.

'A five-minute film-show and a few last words? I'm the son you should have cared for! *Father!*' The ghost had vanished from sight. '*Come back! Father!*

Dad!' The words echoed round the chamber; down the long dark air-shaft where M'Graw had fled. They seemed to echo on in the mountain itself.

But Chegwith Skillett's father had gone. For good.

Chapter Twelve

Chegwith Skillett collapsed. He fell to the floor, and lay there, quite still. For a while, the others tried to rouse him. Then Bette took one arm, and Lankin the other; and Theresa and The Chunterer both took feet; and together – with Jeremy bringing up the rear – they carried the body out of the chamber, out of the mountain and back through the garden (where nothing gave them any trouble, any more). They loaded Chegwith Skillett back into his basket, and then took off.

The Hookeys attacked again, of course. They were swearing revenge, and out for blood. But the Aeronauts flew up into the air, and round, and came at the Hookeys from behind, with a WHOOPS! HIYAAY! PEEP PEEP PEEP! And they shrieked so loudly and shot so straight that they soon had the Hookeys making a hasty retreat.

The friends flew on: three planes and a balloon; while noon briefly brightened, then went cold and grey; while dusk came creeping, then flooding in; they journeyed on, without a word. Chegwith Skillett was lying on the floor. His feet were on the trunk and his arms were by his sides. He was staring at the sky. He had put – it seemed – the whole world from his mind.

And he was crying.

'Sharsskar startar skarrp skarrp trarp!'

Jeremy bent to the mouthpiece. Then, wearily, he shrugged, and turned away.

'Hark! Hark! Creharskar starp!'

'It's on the blink again!' roared Jeremy. 'We've been through all these adventures, and it's still as bad as ever it was! Why can't Lankin *mend* it?'

'You,' squawked a voice, 'are an obstreperous brat.' It was Bette. 'Can *you* always mend things?' Jeremy went quiet. 'There are things – you know – that are just too hard to mend. We're not far from Marta's. I suggest we go down for the night.'

So they did. They landed in the same spot as before, then carried Chegwith Skillett to Marta's, groaning and panting and puffing as they went.

They were almost there when 'Look!' cried Bette.

'How pretty,' sighed Theresa.

'Hm,' said Bette. 'Well, this time you're right.'

A fire was blazing in front of Marta's house. The flames were flickering and leaping high, and tossing clouds of sparks at the darkness above. Marta's little animals were sitting around in a ring. They were humming, crooning, barking and braying in a strange sort of animal song. Some of them were dancing, too. They hopped and skipped

165

and twirled and galumphed, with funny little grunts and squeaks. In the middle of it all sat Marta and The Surveyor. They were looking very pleased, and smiling, shyly. They were also holding hands.

They saw their friends, and jumped up. The Aeronauts lowered Chegwith Skillett to the ground. Then they all hugged Marta and The Surveyor, and The Surveyor and Marta hugged them back.

'Well, Surveyor,' said Bette, at last, 'have you found out what things are about?'

The Surveyor grinned, and looked very bashful. 'I don't think I care,' he confessed, at last.

Marta grinned, too. Then they all of them hugged each other again. When they'd finished hugging,

'Well,' said Bette, 'and now . . .'

'A hotpot!' cried Jeremy. 'A succulent hotpot, for all of us!' So Marta made them a hotpot; and succulent indeed it was. The flyers told Marta and The Surveyor all about their adventures; all about Chegwith Skillett (senior); and what Skillett (senior) had done and said. Then Marta cried for a while, and The Surveyor patted her hand.

But – though Jeremy plied him with hotpot – Chegwith Skillett (junior) did not so much as move.

They carried him into the barn, and went to bed

themselves. They woke the next morning, and he hadn't budged.

'What are we going to *do*?' wailed Bette.

'Easy,' said Jeremy, firmly. 'Chegwith's going home. With me. Everyone says I'm a brat. Well, I may be a brat, but Chegwith's my friend. So I'll help him, somehow. You wait.'

'But they'll put him back in the Home,' said Theresa. 'It'll be worse than ever, with his father gone for good.'

'He won't go back,' said Jeremy. 'I'll see that he doesn't!' he cried.

'I hope you can,' said Bette, in a doubtful voice. Then Lankin took a map from his pocket, and pointed out the route to Jeremy. 'Because we're not coming,' said Bette, at last.

'Aren't you going home?'

'Er . . . no.' Bette clung to Lankin's arm. 'We're tired of all that flying about. We rather like it here, you see.'

'Foresters Anonymous, ahaw!' said Lankin. Theresa and The Chunterer came sauntering up.

'We'll build ourselves houses, like Marta's,' said Theresa. 'Not far away from Marta, or each other.'

'Though not too near,' said Bette, with a cough.

'We'll learn to fish and farm and the like.'

'And we'll be friends to the animals, too.'

'Wn thn,' said The Chunterer. '*Wn Thn!*'

So they lifted Chegwith Skillett back into the

basket. Jeremy hugged them all, one last time. They wished him luck, and a rain-free trip. And then he took off.

The balloon went chugging on its way again. Jeremy stood to one side, and looked out. There were clouds on the distant horizon. He watched them heap and unheap themselves. He thought of M'Graw, the Vanishing Point, Tarkus, the Hordes and Belvedere Jones. He thought of the Dream Machine, as well.

Then he looked round. Chegwith Skillett was standing at his side. For a while, they silently pondered the clouds. At last,

'I hate my father,' said Chegwith Skillett.

'Chegwith,' said Jeremy, 'don't.'

'I hate, loathe, despise and *abominate* my father,' said Chegwith Skillett, brandishing his fists at the sky.

'You'll feel better later,' said Jeremy.

'No I won't' said Chegwith Skillett. 'I'll feel worse. I shall hate him even more than now. He didn't care for anyone, you see. He pretended he did, but he didn't. Not for anyone *real*.'

'Well,' said Jeremy, 'perhaps it made him sad. Perhaps he was really sad, underneath.'

'I don't think he was sad,' said Skillett. 'I think he was cruel and cold. He was interested in people's dreams, but not in people, it seems to me.'

They stared at the clouds. 'And yet . . .' said Skillett, after a while.

'What?'

'I told you, didn't I? *I* used to dream. Of travelling endlessly about the world. Meeting strange people. Seeing strange things. And now . . .'

'Now you can!' cried Jeremy. '*Your* dreams have come true! Some of them, at least! Maybe that's what he wanted, in the end!'

'I have my balloon. My engine and my map. That's enough to begin with. And who knows what may turn up in the future. I used to dream of adventures.'

'You've had some.'

'I used to dream of being brave.'

'You were.'

'I used to dream . . . of friends.'

Jeremy said nothing.

'Of friends. Who were . . . *fond* of me.'

Jeremy whistled, and looked at the clouds.

'Did you mean what you said? That you were . . . *fond* of me?'

'Sort of.'

'What?'

'In a sort of way.'

'That is *not* what you said. Fond as in really, really like a lot. Those were your words, as I recall.'

'I've decided just sort of fond.'

'But you can't!' said Chegwith Skillett, in great agitation. 'Sort of fond isn't fond at all!' He turned wildly about, and faced his friend.

Jeremy was grinning.

'Oh . . . oh . . . oh . . .' said Chegwith Skillett. 'If I were not a gentleman,' (gritting his teeth), 'if I had no respect for the youth of the young . . .'

'Yes?'

'I *should pummel you to death*!!!'

Jeremy smiled. 'But you won't,' he said.

'On the contrary,' said Skillett. 'I think I will.' And he did – well, almost, of course.

At the last, they arrived back home; back above Jeremy's town.

'I shall drop you off,' said Chegwith Skillett, 'and then continue on: CHEGWITH SKILLETT'S WORLD TOUR; or rather, continue with: THE ADVENTURES OF CHEGWITH SKILLETT; to be followed by: THE AMAZING ADVENTURES OF CHEGWITH SKILLETT; FURTHER ADVENTURES OF CHEGWITH SKILLETT; and so on.'

'Are you sure you really have to?' asked Jeremy. 'I've got a tree house in the woods. You can have it, if you like. No one would find you. No one knows it's there.' But Chegwith Skillett shook his head.

'The future beckons,' he boomed. 'Change. Excitement. The great unknown.' He put an arm round Jeremy's shoulders. 'But it's back down to earth for you, young man.'

So they steered themselves back down to earth; back (in fact) to the park where they'd begun. They tied the balloon to a tree.

'And now,' said Skillett, 'let us make an end. Ahem. Of all the companions I could have asked for, you were indeed . . .'

Suddenly, there was a noise of sirens. Flashing lights appeared across the park. The police were racketing towards them. Chegwith Skillett grabbed Jeremy, and leapt back aboard the basket again.

The cars sped up, and stopped. Police got out. There were several men in white coats, as well. In the middle of them all was Humpidore.

'So,' said Humpidore, 'Chegwith Skillett.'

'So,' said Chegwith Skillett, 'old Humpy.'

'*Mr Humpidore to you!*' shouted Mr Humpidore. 'Grab him,' he muttered. 'Quick.'

The policemen edged forwards. So did the men in white coats. Chegwith Skillett took his penknife from his pocket. Then he took hold of the rope.

'Not again!' yelled Humpidore. 'Let's talk!'

'Talk, Humpy?'

'*Mr Humpidore to you!*'

'Er . . . I'm afraid it's not,' said Chegwith Skillett, politely. 'It's what it always was, you know. Old Humpy. Fat Humpy. Ugly Humpy. Dull Humpy. Dumpy Humpy. Stupid Humpy. Bossy Humpy. Bigboots Humpy. Pompous Humpy.' Chegwith

Skillett bent to Jeremy. 'Goodbye, Jeremy,' he whispered. 'I'll be back.' He straightened again. 'Humpy the Soulless. Humpy the Blind. Humpy the Witless. Humpy Unkind. Unfeeling Humpy. Humpy the Rat. But above all, Humpy's a silly old . . .'

Humpidore could bear no more. He threw himself forward, with an anguished roar. The policemen sprang, too. So did the men in white coats.

Chegwith Skillett swung Jeremy clear of the basket. The knife went slicing through the rope. The men all dived . . .

And then – while Jeremy waved and waved until he could wave no more – the balloon went floating, slowly, serenely, up above the telegraph wires, the trees, the chimneys and – in a very short while – the office blocks, pylons and radio masts; back into the great, broad, spacious blue.